MURDER
GO ROUND

D1021083

Books by Carol J. Perry

Murder Go Round

Look Both Ways

Tails, You Lose

Caught Dead Handed

MURDER GO ROUND

CAROL J. PERRY

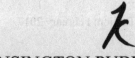

KENSINGTON PUBLISHING CORP.
http://www.kensingtonbooks.com

KENSINGTON BOOKS are published by

Kensington Publishing Corp.
119 West 40th Street
New York, NY 10018

Copyright © 2017 by Carol J. Perry

All rights reserved. No part of this book may be reproduced in any form or by any means without the prior written consent of the Publisher, excepting brief quotes used in reviews.

If you purchased this book without a cover, you should be aware that this book is stolen property. It was reported as "unsold and destroyed" to the Publisher and neither the Author nor the Publisher has received any payment for this "stripped book."

All Kensington titles, imprints, and distributed lines are available at special quantity discounts for bulk purchases for sales promotions, premiums, fund-raising, and educational or institutional use. Special book excerpts or customized printings can also be created to fit specific needs. For details, write or phone the office of the Kensington Special Sales Manager. Kensington Publishing Corp., 119 West 40th Street, New York, NY 10018. Attn.: Special Sales Department. Phone: 1-800-221-2647.

Kensington and the K logo Reg. U.S. Pat. & TM Off.

ISBN-13: 978-1-4967-0715-4
ISBN-10: 1-4967-0715-X
First Kensington Mass Market Edition: February 2017

eISBN-13: 978-1-4967-0716-1
eISBN-10: 1-4967-0716-8
First Kensington Electronic Edition: February 2017

10 9 8 7 6 5 4 3 2

Printed in the United States of America

CHAPTER 1

Late-August days in Salem, Massachusetts, can be quite lovely. Most of the visiting vacationers have left, so driving, parking, walking and shopping is a lot easier for those of us lucky enough to live here year-round. On just such a day, bright with sunshine and with the tiniest hint of fall in the air, my aunt Ibby and I made plans to spend some easy, leisurely, quality time together.

Of course things don't always go exactly as planned.

I'm Lee Barrett—maiden name, Maralee Kowolski—thirty-two, red-haired, Salem-born, orphaned early, married once and widowed young. My sixty-something ball-of-energy aunt, Isobel Russell, and I, along with our cat, O'Ryan, share the comfortable, old family home on Winter Street, where she'd raised me after my parents died.

I sat at Aunt Ibby's round oak kitchen table, enjoying my second cup of morning coffee, while O'Ryan, his big yellow-striped paws on the windowsill, watched a pair of orioles in the garden. My aunt studied the *Salem News*, looking for something "different and interesting" for us to do. "It has to be outdoors," she said. "Winter will be here soon enough."

"Sounds good to me. Anything special in mind?"

She tapped the open page of the newspaper with a neatly manicured fingertip. "Look at this, Maralee. I've always wanted to go to one of these."

I put my cup down and peered at the quarter-page advertisement.

Today Only!
Public Auction of Unclaimed Storage Units.
The Public Is Invited to Participate
In a "Storage War Auction"!
Each Unit Sells to the Highest Bidder.

"How does it work?" I asked.

"Well," she said, "if it works like the TV show, you can bid on a locker and you get everything in it if you make the highest bid."

I knew that Aunt Ibby was fond of watching a cable television program on the subject. She'd often told me about people who'd found amazing bargains by bidding on the contents of abandoned lockers.

"So it's just like a regular auction?"

"Not exactly. You get to peek in the door of the locker. You can't go inside, touch anything or open any boxes. Oh, and it's cash only."

"You pay cash and you don't know what you're buying?" I'd worked in the television industry, both in front of and behind the cameras, most of my adult life. I was currently working during the school year as an instructor of TV production at a local academy.

Even so, I'd never watched that particular show and the pig-in-a-poke concept seemed strange to me.

She shrugged. "Sometimes you can see a lot of the stuff. It's not always in boxes. People come away with wonderful furniture all the time. Antiques. Vintage. Come with me. You'll love it."

She knew she'd hit on my weakness. Aunt Ibby had converted the third floor of the old house into an apartment for me, and I was slowly furnishing it—mostly with antiques and vintage things. "You know me too well," I said. "Where's the auction? What time?"

"It starts at ten," she said, "over near Gallows Hill. If we hurry, we can stop at the bank, get some cash and be there in time."

"Should we put a cap on how much we'll spend?"

"How about we limit ourselves to five hundred dollars?" she said. "Two-fifty apiece?"

My semiretired aunt is nicely set financially, thanks to a combination of old family money, New England frugality, sound investment advice and decades of work as head reference librarian in Salem's main library. A generous inheritance from my parents' estate and the insurance settlement from my race-car driver husband Johnny Barrett's death two years ago, along with my own earnings as an instructor at Salem's newest school, provide nicely for me. We can each afford to take an occasional fling, like the proposed foray into the world of storage wars.

A quick change of clothes—khaki cargo pants and Tampa Bay Lightning T-shirt for me, navy capris and a neat white shirt for my still-slim-and-fit aunt, and we headed for the garage behind the house. O'Ryan peeked from the window—maybe watching us, maybe focused on a lone blue jay. We never know what O'Ryan is thinking. He used to be the pet of a witch named Ariel Constellation. Some say he was her "familiar." In Salem, a witch's familiar is to be respected—and sometimes feared. Unfortunately, I was the one who'd discovered Ariel's drowned body floating in Salem Harbor. Happily for us, my aunt and I were given custody of the quite remarkable, large and beautiful yellow-striped cat.

We decided to drive Aunt Ibby's big, sturdy Buick to the sale, leaving my less practical, but definitely gorgeous, Laguna Blue Stingray Corvette convertible behind. That old Buick's wide backseat and roomy trunk could hold a lot of stuff.

"If we buy anything too huge," I said, "I'll call Pete. He's working nights this week, so I know he'll have time, and he can probably borrow his brother-in-law's truck." Police detective Pete Mondello had become the main man in my life. I knew he'd agree to help out even though he finds my admittedly eclectic taste in home furnishings a little odd.

The parking lot, next to the long, boxlike white building, was more than half filled when we arrived, and Aunt Ibby neatly maneuvered the car into a vacant space next to a chain-link fence. "Looks like the dealers are here," she said, pointing to a row of trucks and vans parked close to the building, a few of them marked with the names of local thrift and vintage stores. "Maybe five hundred dollars won't be enough."

"I think it will be plenty," I said, "and even if we don't buy a locker, it'll be an interesting way to spend a couple of hours."

"I guess you're right. Anyway, sometimes on the TV show somebody wins a really good locker for just a couple of hundred dollars." Her expression brightened. "Besides, I'm sure they have an ATM."

I laughed. "You're incorrigible!" We approached the main gate, joining about thirty people gathered there. Although during my growing-up years my aunt had regularly cautioned me about never speaking to strangers, she'd always avoided following that rule herself. This day was no exception.

"Excuse me," she said, addressing a man wearing a red T-shirt emblazoned with the word *Lucky* in big white letters. "Have you been to one of these sales before?"

"Sure thing," he said. "There's a sale somewhere just about every week. I get e-mails from the auctioneers or see ads in the paper."

"This is our first time," Aunt Ibby confided. "Are most of these folks what you might call 'regulars'?"

He glanced around. "I'd say about half and half. The people with secondhand stores show up all the time. Then there's the ones who come once in a while, just looking for big-screen TVs or old jukeboxes—specialty stuff. There's a few . . . like her." He pointed to a heavy woman, with bright orange hair, wearing a shapeless multicolored dress and blowing a huge pink bubble-gum bubble. "And him"—he indicated a youngish man, in black turtleneck jersey and black jeans, who stood apart from the rest of the group. I remembered seeing the woman around Salem before. That orange hair was hard to miss. Lucky dropped his voice. "They come to a lot of sales and never buy a damn thing. Just watch the rest of us. Kind of creeps me out."

A woman beside him volunteered, "Oh, Lucky, don't be silly. There's a lot of times you don't buy anything. Me too. Sometimes it's just a pile of junk, like, you know, old mattresses, bags of dirty clothes." She made a face. "But sometimes you can really score big-time, huh?"

"You bet. I do okay. Sell most of what I buy on eBay or Craigslist."

The woman wasn't through. "'Course there was that one guy who found a corpse in a barrel." The two laughed.

"Oh, good heavens!" My aunt pressed two fingers to her mouth.

"Is that true?" I asked. "Really?"

"Yep. Man killed his wife. Stuck her body in a barrel. Got away with it too, until his second wife stopped paying the locker rent."

Aunt Ibby interrupted the macabre reminiscence. "Look. There's the auctioneer." She pointed to a blond man wearing jeans and a plaid shirt. He raised his hand and the hum of conversation around us stilled.

"Is everybody ready?"

A chorus of "Yes" rang out.

"Okay then. Listen up. We have seven lockers today. Here's the rules. When we cut the lock, you get five minutes to look around. You can't go into the locker. You can't open any boxes. And whoever has the most money wins it. Let's get started!"

The gate swung open and the crowd pressed forward. My aunt somehow maneuvered us into the front row as a bolt cutter sliced through a padlock and the door rolled upward with a bang and a cloud of dust. It was one of the smaller lockers, just five-by-five, packed with a hodgepodge of mismatched furniture and boxes of varying sizes. Most of the boxes were sealed with tape and lettered on their sides with black marker: TOYS, GAMES, DRESSES. A long one, partially opened, with a discolored and bent aluminum handle sticking out from its side, said POTS & PANS. An oversized, dusty Mickey Mouse plush toy peeked from one side. A few of the larger cartons near the bottom of the pile bore words in a foreign language, with symbols among the letters.

Some of the boxes on that lower tier had popped open at the seams and appeared to contain kitchenware, mostly of the plastic variety. A man behind me stage-whispered, "Doesn't look like much. Dollar store stuff. Chinese. Beat-up crappy furniture. I'll pass on this one."

I heard a bid of ten dollars. A ripple of laughter. Twenty. Thirty. With plenty of jovial encouragement from the auctioneer, the bidding, mostly between the thrift store dealers, slowly went up to 230 dollars. My aunt had scooched down, looking closely at the bottom row. She stood and tugged at my elbow. The bid went to two-forty.

"We're bidding on this one," she said.

"Why? No one seems to think much of it."

"See that kind of tall, scraggly-looking brown box down there? The one with the little tear in its side?"

I peered at the tattered carton she'd described. "With the foreign words on it?"

"Uh-huh. We want it." She spoke so softly I could barely hear, glancing over her shoulder as though she was afraid that someone might be listening.

I laughed aloud. "Okay, but why all the mystery?"

"Shhh." She shushed me and whispered. "You don't understand how these things work. If you act like you see something good, they start running up the bid."

I whispered back. "You're acting exactly like you see something good. What is it?"

Ignoring me, she raised her hand. "Two hundred and fifty dollars."

"Aunt Ibby," I said, "this is the first locker of the day. The ad said there are seven. Maybe one of the others is better than this."

"Two-sixty," came a voice from behind us.

The auctioneer repeated the bids in that amazing, fast-talking, singsongy way they do. "Two-sixty, two-sixty, two-sixty. Do I hear two-seventy?"

"Two sixty-five," said my aunt, using her firm, head-librarian voice intended to discourage all further conversation.

It worked. There were no more bids. For just about half of our budget, we had a five-by-five room packed full of . . . what?

The crowd moved on, some looking back at us with what might have been pitying glances reserved for newbies in the storage wars game. My smiling aunt stood, hands on her hips, surveying the open locker door. "Looks like it'll take us a while to unload all this. We'll start at the top and work our way down to the box I was bidding on."

"Don't you even want to see what's in the other six lockers?"

"Not now. I'm too excited about this one."

"Okay." I know better than to argue with her. Like me, she's a stubborn redhead.

A gray-haired man, pushing a very large four-wheeled dolly and carrying a small stepladder, approached from behind the building. "Looks like you girls might need a little help getting this stuff to your vehicle, eh?" He gave the locker's contents an appraising look. "She's packed pretty tight. I'm Jim. How's twenty bucks sound for moving it out?"

We agreed to the offer and Jim climbed onto his stepladder and began pulling items from the top and handing them down to me. My aunt knelt once more, peering into the torn carton. "Yes," she said, standing and brushing dust from her pants, "I'm absolutely sure now. I can hardly wait to get it home and polish it up."

"Stop teasing," I said. "What is it?"

She looked around, dropping her voice again, as our helper piled boxes onto the dolly, many of them unsealed, and most containing mismatched dishes, plastic-flower arrangements, dingy, wrinkled clothes and the like. Jim topped the load off with a bright green kitchen chair with broken rungs, a scarred maple coffee table and the forlorn Mickey Mouse. "I don't want to open it here," she whispered. "I'll show you later. Want to call Pete now? Looks like we'll be needing that truck. Can't possibly fit all this into the car."

"Couldn't we just take the things you want, and put all the other stuff into that Dumpster over there?" I pointed to a huge green bin. "Doesn't look as though most of this is worth anything."

That comment met with a horrified intake of breath from both my aunt and Jim. "We have to take it all. It's the rules," Aunt Ibby said.

"The rules!" echoed Jim. "And after it's all cleared

out, you have to sweep the floor and take the sweepin's with you too. Them's the rules. And," he added, "you only got today to get it all done."

"And drive it all straight to the city dump," I muttered, shaking my head as I called Pete's private number on my cell. Jim balanced a musty-smelling burgundy velour ottoman and the box of pots and pans onto the dolly, thus exposing part of the bottom row. My aunt lifted the mysterious tall box, clutching it to her chest with both arms.

"Where's your curiosity, your sense of adventure, Maralee? Come on, Jim. Let's grab a couple of those little lamps and start loading the car. My niece will stay here and guard the rest."

The two headed for the Buick—Jim pulling the precariously balanced load with one hand and carrying a shadeless pink ceramic lamp with the other; my aunt walking alongside, one arm hugging her precious box, the other hand steadying the awkward heap.

Fine. Leave me here all alone, protecting a smelly pile of junk. Pacing back and forth in front of the damned locker like a Buckingham Palace guard, I waited for Pete to answer.

"Hi, Lee. What's up?" Just hearing his voice made my mood improve.

"I need to ask a favor, Pete," I began. "Do you think you can borrow Donnie's truck for a couple of hours?"

"I'm sure I can. Why? Have you finally decided to move in with me?" I could hear the smile in his voice.

"Not today," I said, knowing there was a smile in my voice too. "Aunt Ibby and I are at a storage locker auction and we need to transport some . . ." I looked behind me at the open locker, searching for a word. "Some merchandise," I said.

"Okay. Where are you?"

"Thanks, Pete." I gave him the name of the place and he promised to be there with his brother-in-law's truck in twenty minutes.

We loaded the dolly once more, and Aunt Ibby pronounced the Buick filled to capacity. Jim had found an old corn broom among the leftover items, so I began the floor-sweeping process while Jim began piling the remaining artifacts outside the locker. My aunt went in search of plastic bags to hold the sweepings.

"Wonder what's in this one." I leaned the broom against a good-sized wooden crate propped against the rear wall of the nearly empty space. Some of the slats on the top and sides were broken and a few were missing altogether.

"Dunno," said Jim. "Want to give me a hand moving it outside?"

"Sure," I said, pushing the broom out of the way and moving to one end of the thing while Jim positioned himself at the other.

"Okay, miss," he said. "One-two-three, lift!"

The crate was more awkward than heavy, and as we moved together, crablike, toward the entrance, one of the broken slats was exactly at my eye level. As soon as we stepped out into the sunlight, I let go of my end with a muffled scream.

Looking straight at me from inside that crate was another eye.

CHAPTER 2

Jim lowered his end of the crate to the ground—a lot more gently than I had. "What's wrong, miss?" There was real concern in his voice. "Are you okay?"

I couldn't answer right away. I was busy processing what I'd just seen. Or what I *thought* I'd just seen. That corpse-in-a-barrel story flashed through my brain.

"Jim," I said, surprised that my voice sounded so normal, "I'm fine, but do me a favor?"

"Sure, miss. Anything you say."

"Take a look into the crate, will you? Right there. Where there's a slat gone on the side."

"Uh—okay. Here?" He bent and touched the side of the crate next to the missing slat. He used that condescending tone you'd use when speaking to someone you suspect might not have both oars in the water. "You want I should look in this hole, right?" I knew he was trying not to smile.

"Yes. That's it." *You might not feel so smug when you see what I saw,* I thought.

The man jumped backward so fast he nearly landed

on his rear in the dirt. "Holy Mother of God!" he yelled. "There's somethin' in there!"

"What's going on?" Pete had arrived, and Aunt Ibby, clutching a handful of Salem's official overflow trash bags, was close behind him. "Are you all right, Lee?" Pete didn't wait for an answer, but moved quickly, facing Jim and positioning himself between me and the crate.

Jim, his face drained of color, pointed at the wooden container. "In there. It . . . it looked at me." He jerked a thumb in my direction. "Her too, I guess."

"You got a crowbar?" Pete asked.

"In my locker," Jim said. "Hang on. It's right around the corner."

"Get it." Pete peered into a crack at the top of the thing. "Looks like some kind of painted animal. I can see its ears."

"Painted?" I said, feeling like a doofus as I watched Jim scamper away.

"What's in there, Maralee?" my aunt asked. "What did you see?"

I laughed, relieved. "I saw a big brown eye looking back at me. Scared me just a little," I lied. *Scared me a lot!*

Jim returned, still pale, handed a crowbar to Pete, then stepped back against the side of the building. "You gonna open that thing?"

My aunt piled the trash bags onto the floor of the near-empty locker, walked right up to the crate, leaned across the top of it and peeked into the same space Pete had just checked out. "Oh, lovely. I think it's a horse. Open it up, won't you, so we can see, please, Pete?" There was a sound of splintering wood as the sides of the crate came apart.

The thing inside was swathed in a tangle of quilted fabric. Pete tugged at the material closest to the top, partially revealing the owner of the mysterious eye. My aunt was right. It was a horse.

The layered mane was windblown, highlighted with gold leaf, the forelock flipped. A jeweled halter was accented with a single, finely carved rose. The brown eye Jim and I had seen sparkled against the palomino face; and even though the paint was faded, dirty and chipped in places, the wooden horse's head had an air of elegance.

"It's a carousel horse," Aunt Ibby said. "Quite a nice one, I think."

I studied the wooden animal's flamboyant mane and friendly face. How could I have been terrified by such expressive eyes? "He's beautiful," I said. "Let's see the rest of him."

Working carefully, Pete and I unwound the large dirty quilt wrapped snuggly around the horse's body. Aunt Ibby stood close by, offering advice. "Careful now. Looks like some of that dried paint is sticking to the cloth. Oh, dear, that little rose is chipped." Jim sat a judicious few feet away on the top step of the folding ladder.

"Kind of like an equine striptease," I said as the last of the fabric slowly fell away, revealing the wooden horse, straining at his jeweled halter, mane wind-whipped. The right hoof was raised, the flowing tail curved around the rump.

"Looks just like the horses the little kids used to ride on the merry-go-round down at the Salem Willows," Jim offered, leaving the ladder and moving a little closer to the horse.

"They still do," I said. "Only now the horses are made of fiberglass, not carved out of wood like this one."

"Well, let's load up what's left here onto that dolly and put it in the truck." Pete lifted a box full of beat-up, old fireplace tools. I paused for a few seconds, admiring his powerful back muscles moving beneath a Red Sox T-shirt; then I added a rusty frying pan and a framed print of Washington Crossing the Delaware to the pile. "Miss Russell says we have to bag up all the trash and take that home too," he said. "That right?"

"Them's the rules," Jim told him. "I'll start bagging." He reached out a tentative hand, touching a carved bell on the horse's saddle. "You mean somebody *made* this whole horse? They carved it out of wood?"

"Looks that way," Aunt Ibby said. "I'll be doing some research on it." She was already scrolling on her smartphone, so I knew that my tech-savvy aunt was well on her way to becoming a carousel expert. "I'm posting a picture of it," she said. "I'll bet at least one of my Facebook friends knows something about wooden horses."

Within the hour the locker was swept clean, 265-dollar payment made, Jim paid and generously tipped, and the truck bed filled to capacity with assorted junk, plus one fine carousel horse. Pete and I climbed into the front seat of the borrowed truck and prepared to follow the Buick to Winter Street.

"What in the world are we going to do with it all?" I wondered aloud.

"Your aunt says the furniture and lamps and dishes can probably all go to Goodwill. She says she's sure you'll probably want to keep the horse. I guess all the rest, except for a couple of boxes and that one she's been carrying around like a baby, will get thrown out with the regular trash."

"The horse is going straight upstairs to my apartment," I said. "Cleaned up a little, he's going to look wonderful in the living room."

I watched Pete's face. He smiled and shook his head. "If you say so." He pulled the truck into the driveway beside the garage.

Aunt Ibby had already begun unloading the Buick, and three open cartons were lined up in a row on the flagstone walkway leading past the garden to the house. "Hello, dears," she called as we climbed out of the truck. "I think I've found a few more roses among the thorns."

"Keepers?" I asked.

"Keepers," my aunt declared, lifting a brightly colored and oval-shaped item from the box marked TOYS. "Look at this. Russian matryoshka dolls. These look hand carved too. Like the horse." She opened the figure, revealing a smaller doll nested inside, then another and another. "All carved from a single block of wood. Remarkable." She moved to the next carton, the one marked GAMES. "These are chess sets," she said. "Wonderful hand-carved chess pieces, and the other box, the one that's marked 'Dresses,' that one is full of beautiful handmade doll clothes. They've all been wrapped in that special blue paper they use to preserve wedding dresses. And look at this." She held up a heavily carved dark brown wooden clock. "It's a lovely, old cuckoo clock. I've fiddled around with it a little and I think I can get it to work." Arms folded, a wide smile on her face, she surveyed her treasures. "As the woman at the sale said, I think we scored big-time."

"Seems so," I agreed. "Can I have the clock?"

"Of course. I thought you might like it."

"What are you planning to do with the rest of it?"

"I have plans. Don't worry. Pete, as long as you have the truck, do you think you two could drop off the furniture and decorative things at the Goodwill store? We'll just bag up everything else and put it out front with the regular trash tomorrow morning."

"Sure," Pete said. "I don't have to check in at the station until seven o'clock."

Sounded easy. Drop off furniture and décor. Bag up everything else. Of course nothing is as easy as it sounds. It took a good two hours for the three of us to sort and determine exactly what was donation-worthy, and what was destined for the next morning's curbside collection.

O'Ryan, who'd come outside via the cat door, slowed the process by sniffing and pawing at almost every item. Finally, with upholstered items liberally sprayed with a lemony fabric refresher, lamps, coffee table and framed pictures dusted and polished to Aunt Ibby's satisfaction, dishes washed and Mickey Mouse fresh from a trip through washer and dryer, the bed of the truck was packed and ready to roll.

Next came the disposal of the remaining debris. We each donned latex gloves, packed seven bags to the brim with assorted smashed, cracked, defective and fragmented remains of the anonymous somebody's household goods, adding them to the two bags Jim had prepared, and carried the nine full bags to the curb for the next morning's pickup.

The boxes containing the matryoshkas, the chess sets and the doll clothes were stacked in Aunt Ibby's back hall. She'd already carried my clock—along with the mysterious carton that had prompted the purchase of all this—into her kitchen. The carousel horse, with bungee cords loosely securing his dusty fabric wrapping, leaned against the wrought-iron garden fence. In the bright sunlight the grime and chipped paint gave him a sorrowful look and the soft brown eye looked straight at me. Again.

I poked my head into Aunt Ibby's kitchen. "What do you think I should do with my horse? Shall I put him in the garage until I can get him cleaned up, or should I take him upstairs now?"

She snapped her fingers. "I have a wonderful idea, Maralee! From what little research I've been able to do so far, it seems that old carousel horses are often worth restoring. Let's have Mr. Carbone take a look at him."

Paul Carbone was the furniture restorer who'd repaired the tarnished mirror on the bureau in my bedroom. I have a thing about mirrors—and some other objects too. I'd learned fairly recently that I have a unique, and not always welcome, talent. Seems that I'm a scryer. My best friend, River North, calls me a "gazer." River is a witch, and she's one of the few people who know that sometimes, when I look at a reflective surface, I see things that other people can't see. They're quite often things I wish *I* couldn't see either.

"Okay." I shook away the thoughts about mirrors. "Let's call him."

But she was already on the phone, describing the

horse. "About forty-eight inches tall," she said. "A stander. One hoof raised. Paint's chipped and very dirty."

I looked around the neat kitchen. Something new had been added. On the breakfast counter I saw what the mystery carton had contained. It was a tall metal urn, black with tarnish, but unmistakably graceful in its shape. It had a chimney-shaped top and an elegantly molded spigot on one side. My aunt had already polished one spot, where the gleam of sterling silver shone. Curious, I moved closer. In its smooth surface I saw the pinpoints of light, the misty swirling colors that always precede a vision.

I didn't recognize the man. He lay, faceup, next to a little pine tree, sightless eyes wide open, a thin line of blood encircling his throat like a narrow red ribbon.

CHAPTER 3

I closed my eyes, turning my head away. "No," I whispered. "Please, no." It had been nearly a year since the visions, unbidden and unwanted, had intruded in my life. This one, like too many of them, showed me death.

Aunt Ibby's voice seemed to come from a distance, slowly penetrating my consciousness. "Thanks so much, Paul. They'll drop it off at your studio then. Good-bye."

I opened my eyes, daring to look again at the urn. No picture of a dead man marred its surface. Just a tarnished, old piece of silver, with a chimney and a spigot. My aunt, all smiles, faced me. "Oh, you've discovered my treasure! Wonderful, old samovar, isn't it? Sterling. Wait until you see it when I've finished polishing." She crossed the room to the counter and patted the thing as though it was a pet. "I've always wanted one."

I took a deep breath. "Nice," I managed to say. "A samovar, huh?"

"Yes, indeed. It's a beauty. But there's good news about *your* treasure too."

"My treasure?" I tried to block out the image I'd just seen, tried to concentrate on her words.

"Of course, dear. The horse. Mr. Carbone looked at my pictures of it on Facebook and he's sure he can bring it back to its original condition. I told him you'd drop it off after lunch."

There was a knock at the kitchen door. "Come in, Pete," Aunt Ibby called. Pete appeared in the doorway, smiling, his dark hair damp and curling a little over his forehead. "Truck's loaded," he said. "What do you want me to do with Old Paint out there, leaning on the fence?"

"Thank you so much, Pete. The horse goes into the truck too, but he's definitely not destined for Goodwill. Do you know where Paul Carbone's furniture restoration studio is?"

"Sorry, no. Do you, Lee?"

"I'm pretty sure I can find it." I moved away from the counter, from the blackened silver "treasure," which was apparently destined to show me things I didn't want to see. "It's over near the Peabody line, in one of those small industrial warehouses."

"Great." Pete looked in the direction of the refrigerator. "Did I hear somebody say something about lunch?"

"My goodness! Lunch will be terribly late, won't it?" My aunt looked at the clock. "It's nearly three. But don't worry. You two have just enough time to wash your hands while I throw something together."

The laundry room, with its big double sink, was just across the back hall opposite the kitchen. Pete turned on the faucet and filled the shallow side, adding a hefty squirt of detergent. "You first." He took both of my hands in his, lowering them into the sudsy water, then moved the faucet to the deep side of the sink and began scrubbing his own hands. He paused, watching my face. "You okay?"

"Sure," I said, forcing a smile. "Just tired and dirty and hungry, I guess." I located a brush in the cabinet above the sink and went to work on my nails.

"I thought for a minute you looked kind of—I don't know—kind of worried."

"What, me worry?" I gave him my impression of an Alfred E. Newman grin. Pete knows about my scrying. I had to tell him the truth about it. But it isn't something we talk about. I didn't see any point in telling him about the vision in the samovar. We finished washing, dried our hands on the long, cotton roller towel and cleaned the sinks. "Let's go see what's for lunch."

"Smells good." Pete sniffed the air as we hurried across the hall.

The spread on the round table looked anything but "thrown together." Yellow crockery bowls of vegetable soup, thick sandwiches of roast beef and hot mustard on sourdough bread and a frosty pitcher of lemonade— a picture worthy of the cover on a Martha Stewart magazine.

"You're a wonder, Miss Russell," Pete said, helping himself to a sandwich.

Aunt Ibby waved away the compliment. "The miracle of leftovers and the microwave oven."

"It's all delicious. Say, is that thing on the counter

over there what was in the box you've been carrying around?"

"It is," she said, "and wait until you see it when I finish polishing. It's a Russian samovar. Sterling silver. From the late nineteenth century."

Maybe that dead man is from another century. River says the visions can be from the past, present or future.

"Guess it's worth more than you two paid for the locker—and you got Old Paint out there too," Pete said. "Lee says she's going to put the horse in her living room."

"Yes, we scored big-time." Aunt Ibby was clearly pleased with her new phrase. "And you'll see, Maralee. Mr. Carbone will make that old carousel horse look like new."

"I think he's beautiful now. But he'll look happier with fresh paint."

From under the table O'Ryan gave a brief "mmrrow."

"Better be careful," Pete said. "O'Ryan might get jealous, thinking you have a new pet."

I sneaked a bit of roast beef to the cat, who accepted it daintily, then gave my fingers an extra lick. "Never happen," I said. "He knows he's top cat around here."

We polished off the lunch in record time. Even found room for a few homemade sugar cookies. It was a little past four o'clock when we climbed into the truck and set off for the Goodwill store. The horse was secured in the very front of the truck bed, with its head against the rear window of the cab. Whenever I turned to look in Pete's direction, I could see that soft brown eye—no longer frightening—peeking through the glass.

"We might as well go to the Goodwill store in

Peabody," Pete said. "It's just a few streets over from the horse painting guy's place."

"Good idea." We left Winter Street and headed down Bridge Street to Route 114. It was a quiet ride. Pete was silent and I watched the passing scenery, preoccupied with my own thoughts. I felt the truck accelerate suddenly, then slow down. Pete, his stern cop face in place, hit the right-turn signal. Moments later we made an abrupt left turn. He watched the rearview mirror.

"What are we doing? Is something wrong?" I asked.

"Not sure. Thought for a minute we'd picked up a tail. That black Toyota has been behind us since we left the house."

"A 2012 black Camry SE with a rear spoiler?"

He gave me a sideways glance and shook his head. "Yes, my little gearhead. How do you do that? You spotted it too?" He drove around a short block and we emerged once again onto Bridge Street. He checked the mirror. "Must have been mistaken. Anyway, he's gone now."

Actually, I hadn't noticed the Toyota following us, if it even was. "I remember it from the auction," I told him. "A car just like that pulled out behind the Buick when Aunt Ibby left there ahead of us." I didn't bother answering the gearhead question though. Pete knew that Johnny Barrett had been a rising young star on the NASCAR circuit and that I'd spent years hanging around auto-racing tracks. I've even kept up my subscription to *Motor Trend.*

"Probably a coincidence," he said. "There are hundreds of black Camrys around Salem. Popular car." I noticed that his cop face was still in place and that he kept checking the side mirrors. I did too. Thankfully, no Toyota appeared.

We found the Goodwill drop-off station and piled boxes and bags full of the donated debris into a huge white canvas four-wheeled cart, topping off the stack with the newly clean and fluffy Mickey Mouse.

We picked up our donation receipt and returned to the truck, where the horse stood, right hoof upraised, all by himself in the empty bed. "He looks so lonely," I said, "and I'm afraid he'll slide around back there. Do you think he'd fit into the backseat?"

"You'd probably hold him on your lap if you could." Pete smiled. "Backseat's kind of narrow, but we can try. Come on."

We fit the horse into the space behind us without any problem. Old Paint wasn't as heavy as he looked—Pete said he was probably hollow inside. We arranged him at kind of an odd angle with his head sticking out of the small rear window on the passenger side, but I felt better about carrying him that way. The poor thing was already pretty badly chipped and scratched and he didn't need any more abuse. Besides, I liked the way people smiled when they noticed him as we passed by.

We found the rows of industrial warehouses and cruised slowly along the narrow road between them, looking for Carbone's Fine Furniture Restoration Studio. It was at the end of the innermost row of bays, next door to a used-book dealer.

"Welcome, Ms. Barrett." The rotund, smiling man greeted us at the open bright red door, which distinguished Carbone's from its drab, gray-doored neighbors. The smells of varnish, turpentine and paint mixed with the piney scent from a tree-filled lot adjoining the warehouse area.

"Hello, Mr. Carbone," I said. "This is my friend Pete Mondello. Thanks for fitting us in on such short notice."

The two men shook hands. "No problem. I can hardly wait to get started on this project." Paul Carbone moved toward the truck and reached for the open window, touching the horse's mane. "Always wanted to restore one of these. He's small, but he's a pretty one."

"Let's get it out so you can have a good look." Pete opened the rear door. "Want to get the other door, Lee, and push while I pull?" Between us we maneuvered the horse onto the ground. I paused outside the doorway while Pete and the excited restorer carried him into the shop. I turned to follow them inside. A sound, a flash of color from the crossroad at the far end of the monotonous row of doorways grabbed my attention.

"Pete," I said, pointing, "did you see that?"

He joined me in front of the red door. "See what, babe?"

"Never mind. She's gone."

"Who's gone?"

"Nothing. Nobody," I said, feeling a little bit silly. "Let's go in and see a man about a horse."

"Okay." He took my arm and steered me into the shop.

Why shouldn't she be here? Probably lives in the neighborhood, I thought. But it was an odd sight. It isn't every day that I see a very large woman, with bright orange hair, riding on a very small pink motor scooter. I wondered if she'd picked the scooter color to match her bubblegum.

CHAPTER 4

Paul Carbone had clearly been doing some carousel horse homework. A printout of Aunt Ibby's Facebook photos of my horse, along with a couple of watercolor sketches he'd already done from the photos, were pinned to a cork bulletin board hanging above a long, low, scarred and paint-splattered workbench. A copy of *Painted Ponies—American Carousel Art* lay open on a nearby table.

"You've already started work on the project, Mr. Carbone," I said. "How wonderful."

"Please call me Paul, both of you. No need for formality here." He gave a brief wave of one hand, indicating the spartan interior of the place. "As you can see, I don't have a lot of work lined up ahead of yours."

I glanced around. It was true. There was a small three-drawer bureau painted flat black and decorated with hearts and flowers and angels, reminiscent of Peter Hunt's peasant designs from the 1950s. A pair of Victorian rosewood chairs, with needlepoint seat cushions, looked ready for delivery, next to a highly polished mahogany gateleg table.

"Business kind of slow, is it?" Pete asked.

"It's the time of year." Paul shrugged. "Folks'll start fall housecleaning in a month or so, and this place will be packed. I'm not worried. Say, Pete, is it? Want to help me lift this guy up onto the workbench? We'll see what he needs done."

The men placed my horse so that he faced an open window on the right side of the room. A bright fluorescent lamp above the bench illuminated every chip and stain and blemish on the poor creature's wooden body.

I breathed a soft, sad "oooh."

"I know. I know," Paul said, sounding like the sympathetic doctor on one of the medical TV dramas. "He looks pretty bad now, but don't worry, Ms. Barrett—Lee. He's going to be fine."

Pete looked back and forth between Paul and me as though we were both crazy. "Uh, sure. Just fine," he said.

"I think we'll start by giving him a good bath," Paul said, "then I'll get busy sanding that rough paint off. Looks like he's had some pretty bad amateur touch-ups along the way."

"How old do you think he is?" I wondered.

"Hard to tell under all that paint. I'll know more when I get a good look at the construction."

"I can hardly wait to see him when he's finished."

"When my nephews were real little, I used to take them to the Willows to ride the flying horses," Pete said. "They were afraid of the big horses that went up and down. They liked to ride the small one on the inside row that stood still, like this one does."

"Exactly," Paul said. "That's what standers were designed for. The little ones. The fearful ones."

"I know he's in good hands," I said, glancing at my

watch. "Pete, if you have to go to work at seven, we'd better get going."

"Right. And I have to return the truck." He stuck out his hand. "Thanks, Paul. Good to meet you."

"Same here." Paul walked with us to the still-open red door. "I'll call you, Lee, just as soon as I have him all stripped down. Then we can discuss the final finish. Okay?"

"Okay. See you soon." We climbed into the truck and headed for Bridge Street. "Want to shower and change at my place?" I asked. "It'd be faster than you going all the way home first."

"Exactly what I was thinking. Then I can drop Donnie's truck off and pick up my car on the way to the station."

We hadn't planned it, but somehow over the months we'd been together, quite a few items of his clothing were in my apartment and a couple of my outfits were hanging in his closet.

O'Ryan waited for us, just inside the back door. No surprise there. The cat knows unfailingly when someone is coming to the house and he knows which entrance they'll use. We took the back stairway up to the third floor, O'Ryan racing ahead of us. He pushed open the cat door and was already sitting in the middle of the living room by the time we got inside.

Pete paused halfway across the room. "Where do you plan to put Old Paint when you get him back?"

"I kind of see him in front of that bay window," I said, pointing. "Maybe with a lot of plants around him. But I don't think his name will be Old Paint anymore."

"Whatever you say." Pete pulled me close and delivered the kind of kiss that suggested he wasn't in a big hurry to get to work. A series of unfamiliar sounds intruded on the moment. Aunt Ibby had already hung the cuckoo clock on my kitchen wall and it announced, not subtly, that it was six o'clock. "Gotta leave," he whispered.

"I know," I said.

"Don't want to."

"I know."

Pete headed for the shower and I grabbed clean clothes and hurried downstairs to the bathroom adjoining my old, growing-up years, second-floor bedroom. I loved my new digs, but somehow the very girly French Provincial tester bed, the dressing table with ruffled skirt, the white-manteled fireplace and the cushioned window seats still held a lot of appeal too.

Besides, that extra bathroom often came in very handy.

By the time I went back upstairs, scrubbed and shampooed, Pete was dressed and ready for work. Tan slacks, white shirt, no tie. His dark blue sports jacket was draped over the back of one of the Lucite kitchen chairs. He'd started a pot of coffee. Cops drink a lot of coffee. So do I.

"I think we have time for a quick cup before I have to go," he said.

"Good. I love your coffee. Want a sandwich? I have some ham and that Italian bread you like."

"Do you still have that hot mustard?"

"Yep." I put the sandwich together while he poured the coffee. Mine with cream, no sugar. His black.

"I think I'll have to take that sandwich to go." He

looked at the cuckoo clock and picked up his jacket. "I think that damned bird is about to screech again."

"She doesn't screech. She coo-coos." I slipped the sandwich into a plastic bag, gave him a quick kiss and walked with him to the living-room door.

"I'll call you in the morning," he said. "Want to have breakfast with me?"

"Of course I do. What time do you get off?"

"Three a.m."

"Call me a little later than that, okay?"

"Maybe." A smile and another kiss. "Good night."

"You'd better hurry," I said. "Cuckoo's about to announce six-thirty. Call me. But not at three o'clock."

He didn't call me at three o'clock. It was much earlier than that. Barely midnight. I was still awake, sitting up in bed and watching the start of my friend River North's late-night TV show on WICH-TV. *Tarot Time with River North* had become one of Salem's most watched nighttime features. She read the cards for phone callers in between scary, old movies. In a low-cut red satin dress, her long, black braid studded with sparkling silver stars, River looked gorgeous, as always. She'd just announced the night's film offering—*Virus Undead*.

"Creepy zombie flesh," I told O'Ryan, who was curled up beside me. "I think we'll pass on this one." My phone vibrated. I saw Pete's name on caller ID and smiled. "Hi," I said. "Just watching River introducing the movie. O'Ryan doesn't want to see it."

"Sorry to call so late." He sounded serious.

"Something's wrong, Pete. What is it?"

"Maybe something. Maybe nothing. There was a 911 call a little while ago. Sounded like a routine B and E. We sent a patrol car over to check it out."

"Uh-huh. And?"

"It was at Carbone's studio. I'm on my way there now."

"Paul . . . Mr. Carbone? Is he all right?"

"Yes. He's fine. The place was empty. Closed up for the night. I'll let you know what I find out. Just didn't want you to hear about it on the late news. Don't worry."

"Okay." I knew I sounded hesitant. "Please call me as soon as you know anything. I'm wide-awake now. Might as well get up and drink the rest of that good coffee you made."

"I'll call you. It's probably just kids out raising end-of-summer hell. I'll be glad when school starts. I'm just going over there myself because, well, we kind of know the guy. Maybe I can help him with all the damned paper-work this kind of thing involves."

"I'm sure he'll appreciate that, Pete. And if there's anything I can do . . . ?"

"I know. I'll tell him. Gotta go."

I did just what I'd told him I was going to do. Heated up a cup of coffee. Then I put a couple of slices of raisin bread in the toaster and opened a jar of peanut butter. Why not?

My favorite nighttime radio station was running one of those old *Somewhere in Time* Art Bell shows. Art was dis-cussing the possibility of a comet someday hitting our planet.

I hope Pete calls soon. Planet destruction isn't much of an improvement over zombie virus.

I got my wish. The phone rang after only one cup of coffee and one slice of toast.

"How'd it go, Pete? How's Paul doing?"

"Well, we've got kind of a mess here."

"What do you mean? What kind of mess?" I had a very bad feeling.

"Somebody took your horse apart. It's in pieces all over the floor. And besides that, there's a dead guy in the bushes outside the window."

I knew as soon as Pete spoke those words that the dead guy's body was beside a little pine tree and that there was a thin trickle of blood oozing from his throat.

CHAPTER 5

[Faint show-through text from the reverse side of the page is visible but not legible as this page's content.]

Pete was obviously too busy to tell me any more just then, but promised to call as soon as he could. I knew he'd be working well past three in the morning. I tried to process what I'd just heard.

Why is my horse in pieces all over the floor? My poor horse. I felt a wave of genuine sadness. He'd survived for who knows how many years in a storage locker. He'd lasted only a day in my care.

Who is the dead man? Is he the man I saw in the samovar? My head buzzed with questions. I put a second cup of leftover coffee into the microwave and, shivering in the nighttime chill, changed from pajamas to gray sweats. The cuckoo chirped one o'clock. I was wide-awake, with no one to talk to except O'Ryan, dozing on the kitchen windowsill.

I smooshed peanut butter onto the second piece of toast, poured some half and half into the coffee and sat in the chair closest to the window—and the cat. O'Ryan is far from being an ordinary housecat. He's proven that a number of times. So talking to him, even asking him questions, had become somewhat commonplace. My aunt does it too. And sometimes, just sometimes, we get an answer. One that makes sense.

"So, cat," I said, "did you hear what Pete just told me?"

He opened golden eyes and blinked a couple of times. Then he turned his big, fuzzy head and stared out the window.

"Not about the horse," I said. "I know you don't care if my horse is broken. No. I mean about the dead man. The one I saw in the samovar."

He stood, stretched and, giving my hand a fast drive-by lick, trotted across the kitchen toward my bedroom. I followed and clicked on the bedside table lamp. The cat jumped up onto the bed and stood there, facing my full-length, oval mirror on its swivel-tilt cherrywood stand. River is seriously into feng shui, and she'd insisted that the mirror be placed so that I wouldn't see my reflection when I was in bed. I'd relied on her expertise in that matter and seeing my own reflection from the bed had never been a problem. Seeing things I didn't want to see in that mirror—things that weren't even in my apartment at all—had been.

I was reluctant to look where O'Ryan was looking—straight at the mirror, which should have been reflecting the doorway of the room and a bit of the kitchen. The hair along the center of his back stood up, his teeth were bared. He uttered a low growl, then moved aside, making room for me next to him. I sat on the very edge of the bed, stroked O'Ryan's head and forced myself to look at the glass, pretty sure that what he was seeing wasn't anything I wanted to see.

Through swirling colors and pinpoints of light, an

image took shape in the mirror. I recognized the man, and he looked a lot better alive than he had dead. I saw him through the windshield of an automobile. There was one of those little green deodorant pine trees suspended from the rearview mirror and a battered GPS was propped on the dashboard. I leaned toward the mirror, looking closely at his features. Youngish. Thin face, not bad-looking. Short, brown hair. Brown eyes, bright, not sightless now. The vision began to recede, almost like a camera pulling back, expanding the view. I could see the roofline of the black car, the side mirrors, the hood, the distinctive Toyota logo, then the whole car itself. In the background was the long white storage locker building. I saw Aunt Ibby's Buick, the Camry close behind it.

The scene faded. Once again the reflection in the tilted mirror showed the doorway of my room. O'Ryan jumped off the bed and returned to his windowsill perch. I followed the cat to the kitchen, dumped the cup of old, cold coffee, and started a fresh pot. This was going to be a very long night.

So the car that had followed Aunt Ibby was driven by a man who was now dead, his body lying behind a shop where my carousel horse had been taken for repairs. The impact of what Pete had told me about the horse— "in pieces all over the floor"—hit me again. My poor innocent horse! Why take him apart, or chop him up? Something must have been hidden inside. Pete said the horse was hollow. What could be in there worth killing somebody over? And how did it get there?

The cuckoo chirped once. One-thirty.

"Is that all?" I asked the cat, who didn't even open

his eyes. "Only one-thirty? I need to talk to somebody. Besides you." I wasn't about to wake Aunt Ibby. Pete might be tied up for hours, and River wouldn't be through with her show until after two.

I decided that River was my best option. She knew all about the gazing thing, and she was so into the paranormal world that she didn't even think I was weird at all. I grabbed my phone and texted her.

Call me. Even better, come over.

And I waited. More coffee. More peanut butter. By the spoonful. Right out of the jar. I flipped through the pages of the latest issue of *W*. Outfits I liked, but wouldn't buy. Outfits I wouldn't be caught dead in anyway. Gossip about the beautiful people. Cuckoo cycled past two and two-thirty. Maybe Pete was right. She was starting to sound a little bit screechy.

My phone vibrated. Text from River. She was on her way. O'Ryan and I headed down the two flights of stairs to the back door. I didn't unlock it right away. We sat together on the bottom step and waited for her knock. I'd learned the hard way not too long ago that it isn't a good idea to open that door in the middle of the night without knowing for sure who's standing outside.

O'Ryan hopped down from the step and put his paws against the door frame, signaling that River was close. Within a few minutes I heard the crunch of tires on the driveway, the *click-click* of high heels and the long-awaited knock.

"River?"

"It's me."

I hurried to admit my friend. O'Ryan erupted in purrs and mews and promptly entwined himself around her ankles. He loves River. She picked him up, cuddling him against a red-satin-clad shoulder. "Hello, gorgeous cat," she said. "Hi, Lee. What's going on? I didn't even stop to change. It's always something important when you call me late like this. A vision? I brought the cards."

"Come on upstairs," I whispered, being careful not to wake my aunt. "I'll tell you all about it. Thanks for coming."

As soon as the door to my living room closed behind us, River reached into the pocket of the full-skirted dress and pulled out a fat deck of cards. "I know you've had a vision. What was it?"

"I hope you can help me figure out what I saw. Let's sit in the kitchen." She followed me down the short hall and sat in one of the Lucite chairs, placing the deck facedown on the glass top of the table.

"I'll prepare your cards while you tell me what's going on," she said, her expression serious. She removed one card from the deck and handed me the rest. "Here. Shuffle."

I took the chair opposite hers and did as she asked, watching as she placed the card she always uses to depict me—the Queen of Wands—faceup in the center of the table. The queen holds a sunflower in her hand, and lions form the arms of her throne. In front of her is a black cat.

River has read the tarot for me many times. Enough so that I've learned the routine, though certainly not often enough for me to understand how it all works. I placed the deck facedown on the table, then, with my left hand, cut them into three piles. River bowed her head. She was silent for a moment and I knew that she was asking that the higher spiritual forces be present with us. She looked up.

"Okay, Lee. What's going on?" As she spoke, watching my face, she picked up the first pile of cards, then the second, then the third.

Where to begin? So much had happened in one short day. I gave a quick rundown of the storage locker episode, and how we'd wound up keeping the carousel horse and the samovar and getting rid of almost everything else. I told her how Pete and I had gone to see Paul Carbone about restoring the horse, and about my glimpse of a dead man on the surface of the samovar, and of the same man alive and driving a Toyota reflected in the mirror in my room.

"Pete thought a Toyota was following us when we were on the way to Peabody," I said, "and I'm sure the same car followed Aunt Ibby when we left the auction."

River nodded and placed the first card faceup on top of the Queen of Wands. Another card went above the first two, closer to my side of the table. Another, below the first two on River's side of the table. "Then what?" she asked.

"Pete called. It was before I saw the second vision. He says there was a 911 call. Someone broke into Paul Carbone's shop. They did something to my horse—took it apart somehow. And, River, there was a body outside the shop. A man." I thought about those dead eyes, the narrow ribbon of blood on his throat. "I'm sure it was the man in the visions."

She placed two more cards on the table, one to each

side of the ones in the center, forming a cross. "Does Pete know? About you seeing DG in the samovar and the mirror?"

"DG?"

"Dead guy."

"Oh, no. He was in a hurry to get to work and I didn't know then that the man in the samovar had anything to do with . . . anything. The mirror . . . that happened after Pete's call about the break-in. I haven't told anyone except you. And O'Ryan."

The cat, hearing his name, jumped up onto the chair to my right, putting his front paws on the edge of the table. River placed four cards in a row sideways, facing the cat. She put the rest of the deck aside.

"Ten cards," she said. "That's enough. Look." She pointed to one showing a knight on horseback, sword upraised. "Pete's card. The Knight of Swords. He shows up almost every time I read you."

"I remember. That's one of the few cards I recognize." The room was quiet except for the ticking of the cuckoo clock. "What's that one?" I tapped one of the cards facing O'Ryan. "Who's the person in the funny hat with the bubble floating in front of his face?"

"Hey, I have to do this in a certain order." She smiled. "That's the Page of Pentacles. Why? Does it mean anything to you?"

"Maybe the bubble."

"What about it?"

"There was a woman at the auction. She was blowing big pink bubbles. Bubble gum, you know? Then I think I saw her again. She was riding a pink motor scooter over by the warehouse where Paul Carbone has his shop. Before the break-in happened."

"Big woman? Dyed orange hair?"

"Right. Do you know her?"

"Not really. That's Stasia. She's kind of a character around town. Claims she's the lost Grand Duchess Anastasia of Russia."

"That's crazy. She'd be over a hundred years old. Anyway, didn't they find the body?"

She shrugged, moving her hands across the table. "So they say."

CHAPTER 6

River looked from me to the cat and back. "You ready for a reading?"

"I'm ready," I said. O'Ryan didn't comment one way or the other. The golden eyes were focused on River, his ears straight up, alert.

"Okay then." She reached for the card in the center of the table, the one she'd placed across the Queen of Wands. It was numbered 19, a happy-looking card. A big, round sun was shining on a naked child riding on a horse. "A horse," I said. "Cool."

"Not really. See? The card is reversed. Have you lost anything lately? Something valuable maybe?"

I shrugged, puzzled. "Nope. I don't think so. What does it mean?"

"Maybe the rest of the reading will tell us. Something's definitely missing though."

"There could have been something inside my carousel horse. Pete said it was hollow."

She raised an eyebrow. "No kidding? That could be it." She moved on to the card closest to me. It was marked with X, the Roman numeral 10. An old man was seated in front of a castle, surrounded by pleasant-looking people and a couple of dogs. "The grandfather," she said. "This is good. It's all about family and tradition, maybe wealth and property. No worries here."

Next came a card showing a sculptor carving in a church. "This card is about a successful artist. Could be your Mr. Carbone. Looks like your horse is going to be okay." She reached for the card facing her. "Look, Lee. Here's the Moon card. She turns up in your readings almost as much as Pete does."

"That's good, isn't it?"

"Not so much in this position. It's the card of the psychic, and this time it can mean bad luck for someone you know. And, Lee, you may find that your powers are increasing. Pay attention to warnings. Promise?" She reached across the table and touched my hand. "Promise?" she said again.

"Of course." I tried to smile. "No worries."

She smiled too. "Good." She reached for the card beside mine. "And here's Pete. The Knight of Swords. Strong. Brave. Clever. Close beside the queen. That's you."

"I know. And look, he's on horseback too."

"Rushing headlong into battle, as usual. You have a good protector there, Lee, warn him to be especially careful around somebody new in town. You'll see this person too." She picked up the card, looking at it closely. "Maybe somebody from far away."

I don't always understand River's readings and sometimes she's dead wrong. But I do pay attention to her warnings. I promised I'd tell Pete about the new person.

With her left hand, River touched the bottom card of the row facing O'Ryan. "Whew. I don't like the looks of that one," I said. "She creeps me out." The card, marked the 8 of Swords, showed a blindfolded woman, bound with ropes, a fence of swords surrounding her.

River put a hand to her forehead and closed her eyes. I'd seen her do that on her show. I'd always thought that perhaps it was an affectation . . . a made-for-TV move to impress viewers. She had no need to impress me.

Maybe the bound woman creeps her out too.

River's eyes flew open. "Is anyone you know in prison?"

I had to laugh. "No, I don't think so. No jailbird friends at all."

"Don't be too sure. It could happen. If it does, your friend probably isn't guilty. Okay?"

"Okay," I promised. "Could we move on to something more pleasant?"

Cuckoo announced three-thirty. River looked in the direction of the clock. "Where did that come from? Something new?"

"Got it this morning at the storage locker sale. Pete doesn't like it."

"Not sure I do either. I'll check its position, bagua-wise, some other time. You might have to move it." River is my only feng shui consultant. I reminded myself to tell her about my plan to put the carousel horse in front of the bay window in the living room—if I ever got him back.

The next card in the sequence was the Page of Pentacles, he of the floating bubble. "Does this one mean the bubblegum lady is important?"

"I don't think so. No, it has more to do with money, possessions. You'll have some important news, probably from somebody in a high position. That's not Stasia."

"That's good then, isn't it?"

"This is all about choices, Lee. Anytime you choose wisely, it's good." She touched the card directly in front of O'Ryan. I recognized that one. A happy-looking guy, about to step off a cliff. The Fool. "Speaking of choices . . . a brand-new one is in your future. This is a promise of a happy adventure for you." She smiled, and reached for the last of the ten cards.

A yellow-striped paw snaked out and touched the Fool card. Claws out, O'Ryan flipped the card so that the picture faced in the opposite direction. River frowned. "Uh-oh."

I frowned too. "'Uh-oh' what?"

"O'Ryan says I'm wrong. That adventure might not be so happy, after all. Someone could make a mistake that could put you in danger."

"I like your reading better than his," I said. I reached across the table and returned the card to its original position. "He's just a cat. You're the professional. I'm sticking with the happy-adventure scenario."

"Me too," she said. With her left hand she picked up the last card, holding it so that I could see it clearly—and at the same time keeping it out of reach of meddling paws. It was numbered 21 and showed a dancing girl draped in a narrow scarf. "This card is called The World. Some readers call it the best card in the deck, especially when it turns up as the final card in a spread." She reached across the table with her right hand and offered a high five. "I've never had this one turn up for you before. Be happy. You'll get your wish." Her look was questioning. "You thought of a wish before we started the reading, didn't you?"

"Not a wish, exactly," I said. "It was more like a question."

Who is that dead guy and what does he have to do with me?

"That's okay. You'll get your answer." She picked up the cards, stacking them neatly, then leaned back in her chair. O'Ryan returned his attention to the window, where he sprawled out, stretching his full length along the sill. "All in all, things look pretty good for you," she said. "Just the usual advice about being careful, making good choices, paying attention to warnings. I think the visions will become clearer, giving you the answers you need. Moon Mother will take care of that." River stood, smoothing her satin skirt and putting the cards into her pocket. "Almost my bedtime," she said. "Do you feel any better? Did this help at all?"

"Of course it did," I said, meaning it. "Thanks so much for coming over here in the middle of the night. You're such a good friend."

"Hey, I was up anyway," she joked. "You know all about that. You used to work the same hours."

I knew exactly what she meant. I'd done a brief stint at WICH-TV, pretending to be a phone-in psychic. That gig hadn't turned out well. I was glad it was over and pleased that River's show in the same time slot was such a success.

"You're right. But I do appreciate you so much. Come on. I'll walk you downstairs." As we passed through the living room, I mentioned my plans for the placement of the horse, presuming that River was right about Paul being able to restore him.

"Maybe," she said. "When you get the thing back, we'll check it out. And we'll see about the noisy clock at the same time."

With O'Ryan leading the way, River and I tiptoed down the two flights of stairs. I unlocked the door, watching my friend from the back doorstep, with the cat at my side, until she'd waved good-bye and climbed into her car. I put all the bolts, chains and locks in place and returned to my apartment. As I entered, the cuckoo announced four o'clock and, simultaneously, my phone chimed.

"Hello, Pete," I said. "Is Paul okay? What's going on?"

"Paul's okay," he said. "We have an ID on the dead man. Guy from out of town. Strange thing about that though. He had your old boyfriend's business card in his pocket."

CHAPTER 7

My old boyfriend?

Puzzled, I was silent for a long moment as thoughts of a couple of old flames from Salem High School years flashed through my head. *Neil? Ray?*

"Lee? You there?"

"I'm here. Just confused."

"Scott Palmer. That field reporter from WICH-TV. The deceased had Palmer's card in his wallet."

I'd dated Scott a couple of times when I worked at the TV station, but he'd never been in the "boyfriend" category. Far from it. Scott was smart and good-looking, but I'd learned pretty quickly that he was the kind of man who used people. Not my type at all. It didn't seem necessary to explain all that to Pete.

"Have you talked to Scott yet?" I asked.

"No. We'll check with him in the morning."

"Cuckoo says it's morning already. You've had a long night."

"You've got that right. But I'm wide-awake. You still up for an early breakfast?"

"Can I go in sweats and no makeup?"

"Absolutely. That's one of your best looks. I'm on my way. Be there in fifteen minutes."

"Okay. I'll be in the downstairs front hall, on the Winter Street side. Easier than undoing all those locks on the back door," I said. "Just did that when River left."

"River was there tonight?"

"This morning. After her show. I'll tell you all about it when you get here."

And you'll tell me all about my ruined horse and the dead guy in the bushes and what Scott Palmer has to do with anything.

I wasn't exactly honest about the no makeup thing. A tiny bit of mascara and some pale pink lip gloss improved on nature without being too obvious. O'Ryan and I crept down the two flights past Aunt Ibby's room, me with sneakers in hand, O'Ryan on little cat feet, being careful to walk on the outer edges of the treads. (A trick I learned in college sneaking in after curfew. The edges of an old stairway don't creak like the centers do.)

Within minutes, O'Ryan said "mmrup," put his front paws against the bottom of the long window beside the front door, signaling that Pete's car had turned the corner onto Winter Street. How does he do it? I don't know, but he's always right.

The unmarked Crown Vic rolled to a quiet stop. Disabling the alarm system, I opened the door, gave the cat a good-bye pat, hooked up the alarm again and hurried to the curb.

"Good morning," I said, leaning across the center console for the expected kiss.

"That's strange," he said, looking past me toward the

house. No kiss. No "good morning." Just his cop face. Cop voice too.

I followed his gaze and saw . . . nothing. "What's strange? I don't see anything."

"That's it. Nothing. Where's all the trash we put out there yesterday? There are barrels and bags in front of almost every house on the street. That means the collection truck hasn't been here yet."

He was right. Somebody had grabbed all that nasty, old junk we'd thrown away. "Why would anyone want it? Anything remotely useful went into the house or to Goodwill. The stuff in those bags was totally worthless."

"Somebody doesn't think it's worthless," he said. "Somebody thinks there was something valuable in your storage locker. Maybe they thought it was inside that hollow horse. Maybe even something worth killing over."

"The DG?"

Pete frowned. "DG?"

"Dead Guy. River made it up."

"Looks as though there might be a connection. I'll run it by the chief."

"You said that the man had Scott Palmer's card. Do you think that Scott's connected to . . . to whatever this is all about?"

He smiled then, a real smile. Cop face gone. "Seems like quite a stretch, doesn't it? Anyway, you want to know about Old Paint."

"I do," I said. "But that's not going to be his name. You said he's in pieces? A lot of pieces? Or just a couple?" I tried to visualize the scene. Was he split in two like a chicken breast? Or was he in tiny bits all over the floor?

"According to Paul, the horse was taken apart just

about the way he was put together. Apparently, the body, legs and tail were all carved separately in halves. The head was one separate piece."

"So you mean he can be put together again?"

"Just like Humpty Dumpty, babe. Of course he'll have to replace all the stones with new ones."

"Stones? The jewels in the halter?"

"Somebody pried them all out. Maybe the crooks thought they were real."

"Were they?"

"Of course not. Just glass. What was left of them was colored dust."

We'd pulled up in front of our favorite early-morning restaurant. No name out front. Just a plain, old, two-story house with a flashing neon OPEN sign in one window. "You hungry?"

I was, and said so. As soon as we stepped inside, those good New England breakfast smells turned hungry to ravenous. We slid into a high-backed booth close to the rear of the room. Two mugs of steaming coffee appeared on the table almost instantly.

"What'll it be, kids?" The smiling gray-haired waitress stood ready with her order pad. "Specials are on the blackboard."

I ordered a veggie omelet, whole wheat toast and bacon. Pete chose ham and eggs, with a side of pancakes. I dumped three creams into my coffee and waited for him to start talking. I knew he couldn't say much about police business, but since we both knew Paul—and my horse had been vandalized—I figured he'd have something to share with me. Besides that, I knew I'd have to tell him about that man in my mirror.

"The deceased had an Illinois driver's license." Pete kept his voice low, even though there were few patrons in the place yet, and none within hearing distance of us. He picked up his mug, took a gulp of coffee and looked at me expectantly.

"Oh, come on," I whispered. "Is *that* all you're going to tell me about the murdered guy? What did he die from?"

"Upper-body trauma," he said with a straight face.

"I guess that would include his throat." I kept my tone even.

That got his attention. He frowned. "Been seeing things?" That's how Pete always refers to the "gift" I have, "seeing things."

I nodded. "Uh-huh. Since yesterday morning. I didn't mention it because it didn't make any sense. Didn't seem to relate to anything." I paused as our breakfasts arrived, our coffees refilled, then continued. "It relates now for sure."

"Want to tell me about it?"

I described what I'd seen in the samovar. "He was next to a little pine tree. His eyes were open, Pete, and"—I touched my throat—"there was this thin red line . . ."

He reached for my hand. "I know." Of course he knew. He must have seen the same thing.

"Then I saw him again tonight. Alive. He was in the big mirror in my room."

"Alive?"

"He was driving the Toyota. The black Toyota that followed Aunt Ibby after we left the auction."

"You were right about that too," he said. "We found

the car. It was back in those woods next to the warehouse complex."

I know Pete's not comfortable with my "seeing things." Actually I'm not comfortable with it either. Who would be? It's weird and creepy and I wish I couldn't do it. But I have to admit that sometimes—just sometimes—it's been a really handy "gift" to have.

"About the red line—can you, do you want to—tell me what caused it? I mean, why is he dead?"

"We don't have the ME's report yet. My guess? A garrote of some kind. Whoever it was surprised him from behind."

We both grew quiet, concentrating on our food. Questions buzzed around in my head. His too, I guess, because in his cop voice he said, "I'd sure like to know what became of all that trash we put out last night."

"Well," I offered weakly, "I know some people go around collecting stuff from trash that can be repaired."

"Yeah, sure. Things like vacuum cleaners and chairs and old TVs. Not sealed-up bags that they can't even see into. Not nine of them!" He shook his head. "Must have had a truck. I wonder if any of the neighbors have surveillance cameras that might have caught the action."

"Could be," I said. "It's not against the law anyway, is it? Taking other people's trash? If it is, I'm guilty." I raised my right hand.

"You are?" He tried to hide a smile. "What'd you take?"

"You know that cute, little shabby chic footstool I use to reach the shelf over the refrigerator?"

"Kind of washed-out blue with chipped paint?"

"Right. It's adorable. Probably would have cost forty

dollars in a vintage shop. Got it free. On a curbstone right down the street." I stuck out my chin. "So arrest me."

"That's different, you little goof." He smiled then. "But no kidding, I wonder what they're after—and if it's the same thing the guy outside Paul's shop was looking for. Maybe they both thought whatever it is was inside the horse. I'm betting it wasn't."

"And what about all the leftovers we took to Goodwill? Do you think they followed us over there? Got those things too?"

He looked at his watch. "Only five-thirty. Too early for Goodwill to be open and I've got to get some sleep. Probably working late again tonight. Maybe later I'll take a ride over there. Check and see if anyone showed an interest in our load of junk."

"I could do that."

"No. You just leave it alone."

"Uh-huh." I made a little sandwich with half a slice of toast and the last couple of strips of bacon and didn't make any promises. "I've been thinking about that business card."

"Palmer's card?"

"Right. Where did you say the dead man's license was from?"

"Illinois."

"I'm pretty sure Scott told me that he'd worked at an Illinois TV station once. Did sports. That's probably the connection."

"Probably. I'll check it out later today."

Breakfast finished, table cleared, savoring one last cup of coffee, I leaned back in the booth, watching Pete's face. "You look tired," I said. "Can't one of the other detectives talk to Scott? And, Pete, River told me to be sure to tell you to be careful around somebody new in town. Okay?"

"I'm always careful. Don't worry about me. I've been doing this a long time. I'll go back to my place and take a nice power nap and by noon I'll be ready to roll." He leaned forward. "You, on the other hand, don't look tired at all. You've been up all night too, and you're as gorgeous as ever."

Not true, of course, but I liked hearing it anyway. "Well, then. Shall we both try to catch up on missed sleep?" I slid out of the booth. "If you're buying, I'll get the tip."

"Deal," he said, and headed for the cash register while I fished in my handbag for the appropriate amount, plus a little extra because I love the place.

When Pete dropped me off in front of the house, I noticed that trash collection had begun on Winter Street. I also noticed that when the truck stopped several houses away, the Crown Vic stopped too. Pete got out and spoke briefly with one of the men handling the bags and barrels.

Aunt Ibby was already up, dressed and working on the *Boston Globe* crossword when I popped into her kitchen to wish her good morning. O'Ryan was there too, enjoying his favorite morning kibble from his special red bowl. "You're up and about early, Maralee," my aunt said. "Got time to have a cup of coffee with me?"

"I've had so much coffee already, I'm fairly sloshing with every step," I said, "but I'll sit and watch you drink yours."

She put down her pen. (Yes, she does the crosswords

in ink.) "You were up pretty late. I heard River leaving in the wee hours."

"Oh, Aunt Ibby, I'm so sorry. We tried to be quiet."

"You didn't wake me, dear. It was O'Ryan, the silly boy. He insisted that I follow him to the front window just to watch the city men collecting our rubbish."

CHAPTER 8

"What time was that?" I asked, knowing that the *official* trash collection had barely just begun on Winter Street.

"It was around fourish," she said. "Just before River left."

"Was it one of the big rear-loader trucks?"

"No. It was one of the smaller ones, a van type, now that you mention it. Why?" She cocked her head to one side. "What difference does it make? What's going on?"

"There's quite a lot going on," I told her. "And some of it seems to involve our nine overflow trash bags."

"This doesn't sound good." She folded the newspaper and put it aside. "What's happened?"

"I guess I'd better start at the beginning." I told her about the vision I'd seen in the samovar. "I knew the man was dead, but I didn't recognize him. I had no idea what it meant. Then he showed up again in the big mirror in my room, but this time he was alive. And, Aunt Ibby, he was driving a black Toyota. I'd seen the car before. It was right behind your Buick when you left the storage locker sale."

"Good heavens, child! Why didn't you tell me about it?"

"I'm sorry, but it didn't seem to mean anything at the time."

"Is that why you called River? To tell her about the visions?"

I nodded. "There's more. Pete called to tell me there'd been a break-in at Mr. Carbone's shop."

"Oh, dear. Is Paul all right?"

"Yes. He's fine. He wasn't there. But somebody took the carousel horse apart and, Aunt Ibby, there was a dead man outside of the building. I'm pretty sure he was the man in my vision."

"Were the police able to identify him?"

"Yes. Pete couldn't tell me his name yet, of course, but it's the strangest thing! He had one of Scott Palmer's cards in his pocket."

"Your reporter friend from WICH-TV?"

"Uh-huh. The dead man was from Illinois and I'm quite sure that Scott once told me that he used to work at a station there. That probably explains the card."

"Probably. I certainly hope it's nothing more sinister than that. Now tell me, please, what all this has to do with our rubbish."

"Pete will want to talk to you about that van you saw. Whoever it was didn't take anyone else's trash. Just ours. Pete says that somebody must think there was something valuable in our storage locker." I hesitated for a moment before repeating the other thing Pete had said. "Something worth killing over."

She frowned. "I can't imagine what it could be. We got a few very nice pieces, it's true, but nothing of really great value."

"Pete and I were wondering about the things we took over to Goodwill. Wondering whether anyone went there, looking for whatever it is too."

She looked at her watch. "It's still a bit early. Do you think we should take a ride over there later, just to see if anything's missing?"

"That's exactly what I was thinking."

"Perhaps you'll want to change your . . . um, outfit."

I looked down at my old gray sweats. "Sure thing," I said. "I'll shower and change. What time do you think they open? Around nine?"

"That sounds about right."

"Let's take my car," I said. "Leave at eight-thirty?"

"Eight-thirty it is."

We were on the road by eight thirty-five. Convertible top down, morning sun in our faces, wind in our hair. If it wasn't for a dead guy's face on a samovar, my poor broken horse on Paul Carbone's shop floor and some creep stealing our trash, it might have been the start of a really nice day.

The Goodwill people were just unlocking their front door when we pulled into the parking lot. "Looks like we're the first ones here," Aunt Ibby said.

"Good. We brought the stuff over fairly late yesterday afternoon. They wouldn't have had time to sell much of it yet."

"I have a pretty good idea of what we sent over here. I think I'll notice if anything's missing."

"It was a lot of odds and ends. They probably don't even have it all sorted out, tagged and put out for sale yet. What are we going to tell them we're looking for?"

She gave a broad wink. "I've found it's usually best to tell the truth. At least as much of the truth as possible." She climbed out of the car and led the way to the store.

The bell over the door tinkled a welcome and a woman behind a glass-topped counter wished us a "good morning." I nodded and let my aunt do the talking.

"Perhaps you'll think this is an unusual request," she began, "but we donated quite a few items yesterday and we wonder if you'd let us take a peek at the things we sent."

"Not unusual at all. People are always leaving wallets or rings or letters or cash among the old clothes and cups and saucers. Do you have your receipt?"

I fished in my purse. "Got it." I handed over the wrinkled slip and glanced around the jam-packed, cavernous room, convinced that no matter what in the world anyone might ever want or need, it would eventually show up in a Goodwill store. So far, though, nothing in this one looked familiar.

The woman peered over half-framed glasses. "Oh, my. That donation. I'm going to let you speak with the manager." She hurried away from the counter and disappeared down a long aisle between rows of garment racks. Aunt Ibby and I shrugged our shoulders simultaneously and looked at each other.

"What was that all about?" I whispered.

"I can't imagine. Look. Here comes the manager. I know her." My aunt moved forward, extending her hand. "Hello, Grace. You're looking good. This is my niece, Maralee. Maralee, my friend Grace Foster. Is there some sort of problem with our donation?"

The woman and I exchanged mumbled "how-do-you-do's" and she motioned for us to follow her past racks of T-shirts, jeans and scrubs to her office at the rear of the room. "Come in, come in." She closed the door behind us and indicated that we should sit in a pair of blue upholstered club chairs, while she remained standing behind a large gray metal desk. "This is a most unusual circumstance," she said. "All of the items you donated are already gone."

"Gone?" my aunt said. "Gone where?"

Grace Foster spread her hands apart in a helpless gesture. "It's a bit of a mystery, Ibby. Right after the people who left the items drove away, a woman on a motor scooter rode right up to the canvas cart and started pulling things out before we'd had a chance to check them in."

"Stasia," I said.

"Yes. Stasia Novikova. Do you know her, Maralee?"

"No. My friend knows her. I've seen her around Salem from time to time."

"Stasia's a bit . . . odd. The attendant asked what she was looking for. She mumbled something about doll clothes, pulled a few more things out, said she was sorry and rode away."

"If this Stasia person didn't take anything, then where has it all gone?" My aunt was beginning to sound a little bit cranky.

"After Stasia left, a van pulled up and two men got out. They went over to the very same cart, picked up a couple of items, and offered the attendant two hundred dollars in cash for the whole thing. He ran inside and got me. By the time I got out there, they were already putting things into their van. What nerve!"

Aunt Ibby gasped. "I should say so! What did you do?"

"Well, they were quite intimidating men, if you know what I mean. And the contents of the cart looked pretty shabby to me. No offense intended to your donation, Ibby. And, besides, two hundred dollars can do a lot of good, so I accepted their offer."

"No offense taken, Grace. So they just loaded up all our stuff and drove off with it?"

"At first they drove out behind the building. They stopped for a few minutes out there next to our Dumpster."

"They bought it and then threw it all away?" I asked.

"Oh, no. Not all of it, by any means. But the saddest thing was . . . oh, dear . . . it was really rather frightening."

"Why? What happened?"

"I watched from here." She gestured toward the window and pulled aside oatmeal-colored draperies so that we could see the big green trash bin at the back of the property. "After they'd left, after I was absolutely sure they'd gone, I went outside to see what they'd disposed of."

We waited expectantly for her answer. Her tone was hushed, and she closed the draperies. "It was mostly old pots and pans, plastic dishes and such, but the sad thing was poor Mickey Mouse. They'd taken a knife or a razor or something to him and slashed him to pieces. Pulled all his stuffing out. Even cut off his ears."

We were all silent for a moment; then my aunt spoke. "Grace, do you happen to recall what color that van was?"

Grace Foster looked thoughtful. "I believe it was gray. Maybe silver. It badly needed washing. I remember that."

Aunt Ibby nodded. "Did it have those big doors on the side, like some of them do?"

"Yes, indeed. And the two of them just grabbed things out of the cart and shoved it all into that dirty van as fast as they could."

I knew that Aunt Ibby was thinking about the van she'd seen in front of our house early that morning. "Think it was the same one?" I asked.

"I'm sure it was." She stood, facing the store manager across the desk, and I got to my feet too. "Thank you for your help, Grace. We'll be going along now. Good to see you. The store looks lovely."

"Ms. Foster," I said, thinking of what Pete would say if he was here. "Do you happen to have security cameras outside the building?"

"Yes, we do. Why? Do you think those men have done something wrong?"

"It doesn't seem as though they've done anything illegal," I admitted. "But could you save the video for a few days? Just in case the police might be interested?"

She looked doubtful, but agreed anyway. We three exchanged the usual parting pleasantries and I followed my aunt through the crowded aisles and outside into the sunshine.

"What do you think about all that?" I could tell that

Aunt Ibby was intrigued by what we'd learned. I was too. "Quite a lot to take in, isn't it? First someone follows you home from the sale, then the Stasia woman follows Pete and me to Paul's shop, then two men in a van follow her to Goodwill. Where does it all lead?"

"You know what, Maralee?" She gave me one of her wise-old-owl looks as we climbed into my car. "Strangely enough, it makes me think of a carousel, going around and around, with none of the horses ever catching up with the one ahead of him."

CHAPTER 9

Even after we got home to the house on Winter Street, I couldn't seem to shake Aunt Ibby's carousel analogy. We were both quiet as I put the top up and pulled into the garage. I locked the 'Vette, then pulled the door handle of the Buick, making sure it was locked too.

Aunt Ibby gave me a questioning look. I realized that I was being just a tad paranoid, and shrugged my shoulders, giving a short, unfunny laugh. "Can't help it," I said. "I can't help feeling kind of—well, *violated*. I know that all those guys took was trash we didn't want, and they didn't even step on our property to do it. I think it's more being followed that's got me spooked."

I made sure the garage doors were locked too, and we started up the path to the house together, passing my aunt's carefully tended garden. Tall sunflowers still bloomed there, and blue morning glories twined around the wrought-iron fence, where the wooden horse had so recently leaned. O'Ryan waited for us in the back hall, and greeted us with enthusiastic purrs and "mrrows."

He did figure eights between us, rubbing soft fur against our ankles.

"It's lovely to get such a warm welcome home, isn't it? How did we ever get along without you, O'Ryan?" She bent to pat the cat. "Are you coming in, Maralee? Or going right up to your apartment?"

"I think I'll go on up. Have some housecleaning waiting up there for me, and since school starts in a couple of weeks, I have some prep work to do for my classes. And," I glanced at my watch, "I think I need to call Pete pretty soon to tell him about what we learned this morning." I unlocked the door to the two flights of stairs leading to my place. The cat darted ahead of me. "Looks like O'Ryan plans to help."

By the time I arrived in my living room, O'Ryan was already seated on the couch, grooming his whiskers. He has the convenience of a cat door and seems to take great pleasure in being the first one home. There's another cat door in my kitchen entrance, which opens onto the third-floor hall. From there our lovely, old polished oak staircase curves its graceful way down the two flights to the main foyer and the front-door exit on the Winter Street side of the house—in stark contrast to the unadorned and narrow back stairs the cat and I had just climbed. There are more stairs, leading from the third floor up to the attic, but that's a climb I rarely take. Bad memories from up there. Really bad ones.

Once inside, I gave the bay window an appraising look, picturing once again how the horse might look there, surrounded by greenery. This time, though, in my imagination, he was fully restored, his colors vivid, his windblown mane bright with golden highlights.

O'Ryan looked in that direction too, but who knows what cats see? Especially that one.

I hadn't been kidding when I'd told Aunt Ibby I had housework to do. I ran my fingers across the top of the Mission-style oak barrister's bookcase where, behind glass panels, I housed my textbooks from Emerson College, the set of World Book Encyclopedias my aunt had given me when I was in first grade, and my Sue Grafton mysteries, *A* through *Y*. I found dust. Quite a lot of it. Old houses like ours tend to be dusty, but even so, this was a bit much.

My collection of bronzed figural pencil sharpeners were arranged in an orderly row across the top of the piece. I'd been collecting them since I was eight. It was Aunt Ibby's idea. They're quite inexpensive, there must be a thousand different designs, they're found in just about any antiques store, and the hunt had kept me quietly occupied while my aunt dragged me around from shop to shop. There were about fifty of the little metal sculptures in my display. I picked up a miniature Empire State Building. It needed dusting. They all did.

"Come on, cat," I said. "We've got work to do."

He gave me a don't-be-silly look, stretched, turned to face the other side of the room and went to sleep. Or at least gave a good imitation of a sleeping cat. I tiptoed out of the room, down a short hall past the linen closet and bathroom and into the kitchen.

I love my kitchen. It looks efficient, thanks to the appliances Aunt Ibby had installed before I'd even seen it. But she left the furnishings and decorating up to me, so it looks exactly the way I want it to. My table and chairs are clear, beautiful Lucite, circa 1970. Some of the cabinets have glass doors to display vintage Russel Wright china and 1950s Pyrex bowls. River told me once that I needed a picture of fruit to balance the energy and that's grown into an arrangement of small antique watercolor paintings of berries and veggies on the northeast wall. My aunt had hung the cuckoo clock just next to the entrance to my bedroom.

I sat at the table and looked around, satisfied. "It's almost perfect," I told myself aloud. "Now if I could just learn to cook . . ." You'd think that after spending my formative years with Aunt Ibby, some of that talent might have rubbed off. Didn't happen. With a sigh I opened the under-the-sink cabinet, pulled out a few spray bottles and a new roll of paper towels and got to work.

By the time the cuckoo announced noon, the dusting, sweeping, mopping and polishing chores were about half finished. Feeling virtuous, I took a break, poured a tall glass of sweet tea—a habit I'd picked up when I lived in Florida—cut myself a thick slice of Aunt Ibby's chocolate chip banana bread, sat on a stool at the counter and speed-dialed Pete's private number.

He picked up right away. "Hi. Do you miss me already?"

"Of course I do. Didn't wake you, did I?"

"Nope. Had a real power nap. Good thing because the chief's got us all working overtime on the new case at Carbone's. Thought I'd take a ride over to that Goodwill store before I clock in."

"Sure. Well, look. Aunt Ibby and I might have . . . um, saved you some time on the Goodwill thing," I said, knowing as soon as the words were out of my mouth that he wasn't going to be happy about it.

He wasn't. He used his I'm-trying-to-be-patient cop voice. "Could you be more specific about that?"

So I blurted it all out. I began by telling him about Stasia looking through the cart as soon as we'd left. "She said she was looking for doll clothes, but apparently she didn't take anything."

"Wait a minute. Who the hell is Stasia?"

"I guess you didn't see her at the storage locker sale, did you? Big woman. Orange hair. Rides a pink scooter."

"Oh, yeah. Local character, harmless. What else?"

I told him, in as much detail as I could remember, what Grace Foster had said about the two men in the van buying the whole lot for two hundred dollars. "They even slashed the Mickey Mouse. Tore out his stuffing," I said. "But, Pete, the store has outdoor security cameras and I asked her to be sure to save the videos for you."

His "that's good" was gruff. "Obviously, something from that locker is worth a lot to somebody."

"Aunt Ibby thinks the van was the same one the men who took our trash used."

"Not too surprising. I'll come by later and talk to her about that. First I have to see what the ME has to say about the victim and find out what forensics has found at the scene and in that Toyota," he said. "And I'll send a uniform over to pick up that video and what's left of Mickey Mouse."

"Okay. Well, maybe I'll see you later then."

"Sure thing. Gotta go now."

By this time the nosy cat had given up pretending to sleep. He strolled into the kitchen, hopped up onto the windowsill and sat, watching me. I sighed, drank the last of the tea, put the dishes into the dishwasher, got a new roll of paper towels and prepared to resume cleaning.

"Come on, big boy," I said. "You can at least keep me company." I put the roll of towels under my arm and wheeled the vacuum cleaner into the living room. I know most animals don't like the sound of the vacuum, but O'Ryan doesn't mind it at all. He also likes thunderstorms and enjoys watching lightning from the kitchen window. Go figure.

It didn't take too long to put the living room to rights. It's the least-used space in the apartment. The finishing touch was the careful replacement of the little pencil sharpeners on top of the bookcase. Without warning, and with a leap that looked like slow motion, O'Ryan landed on all fours—smack in the middle of the arrangement—without knocking over a single tiny coffee mill, U. S. Capitol Building or bust of Lincoln.

"Nicely done, cat," I told him. "Now let's see if you can get down from there as gracefully as you got up." With a snooty tilt of his head, O'Ryan, lifting each paw delicately, reversed direction, became airborne and made a soft landing on the carpet. So did my Statue of Liberty, a souvenir of a high-school class trip to New York City.

"Good for you that these things are darned near indestructible," I told him, replacing Lady Liberty on top of the bookcase. "You might at least look apologetic about it." Unremorseful, he swished his tail and trotted back toward the kitchen while I headed for the bathroom and a nice, long shower-and-shampoo session.

I emerged half an hour later, body clean, relaxed and lotioned, red hair damp and much too curly, mind focused on school prep. Barefoot, dressed in faded jeans and a NASCAR sweatshirt, I spread textbooks, file folders, yellow legal pad, sharpened number-two pencils, a fresh cup of coffee and my laptop on the kitchen counter. I was prepared for serious work.

The previous year my classes had covered TV production and we'd produced an award-winning documentary about the long history of the building where the school was located—the long-vacant Trumbull's Department Store. The curriculum had been expanded this year to include investigative reporting. I looked forward to it. I'd come to enjoy my fairly new career as a teacher just as much as I'd enjoyed my years in front of the camera as a weathergirl, a shopping-channel host and, of course, my rather inauspicious and short-lived stint as a phone-in psychic. With Pete's encouragement, I'd also been taking an online course in criminology. I found that I liked learning about why criminals behave as they do.

For instance, why would someone steal somebody else's trash—or murder an innocent Mickey Mouse?

"Don't be silly," I told myself aloud. "Neither of those things count as criminal behavior." I thought about the dismembered Mickey. "Clearly, they're looking for something. But what?" There was real criminal behavior going on at Paul Carbone's shop though. A man had been murdered.

They not only looked inside a stuffed toy, but they looked inside a wooden horse. Did they find whatever it is?

I tried hard to dismiss the distracting thoughts, to concentrate on the creation of my lesson plan for "Introduction to Investigative Reporting." The Tabitha

Trumbull Academy of the Arts—named for department
store founder Oliver Wendall Trumbull's wife—better
known around Salem as the Tabby, is what the brochures
refer to as an "educational enhancement" institution.
Located in the revamped old Trumbull's Department
Store, it's now a professionally staffed school where students of all ages can pursue their dreams of dancing,
painting, acting, singing, writing and, in the case of my
classes, TV production and performance. There are no
entrance requirements, no final exams and no degrees
offered, but so far a significant number of Tabby grads
had achieved success in their chosen artistic endeavors.
One of my students from last year's class, Therese Della
Monica, already had a part-time job as call screener for
Tarot Time with River North, and one of the summer program acting students, Daphne Trent, had signed a
Hollywood movie contract!

I'd just begun making notes on the importance of
developing reporting skills when I began feeling a little
bit nervous about teaching this particular subject. After
all, even though I'd taken a semester on the topic at Emerson, I'd never done any actual investigative reporting
myself. Oh, I'd wanted to. Just never had the opportunity.

Make the opportunity. You can learn along with the class,
I thought.

O'Ryan chose that moment to jump up onto the
empty stool next to me. "What do you think, cat? I know
the basics. I've seen it done, working in different TV
stations. And I have all these textbooks." I pointed to the
volumes stacked on the counter. "Look. *Fundamentals of
Investigative Journalism, Understanding the Freedom of Information Act, Social Media Tools in Investigative Reporting.*

I even have Barbara Walters's *How to Talk with Anybody About Practically Anything*."

Propping big yellow-striped paws on the edge of the counter, O'Ryan looked back and forth between me and the assembled materials. After a long moment he leaned toward me and gave my elbow a pink-tongued lick. I took that as affirmation of my teaching ability, and for some crazy reason, it actually made me feel much better about the whole lesson plan thing.

I scribbled away on the yellow pad, barely counting the intermittent "coo-coos" issuing from the clock on the wall. My coffee was cold and my bottom numb when I finally stood, stretching cramped muscles, satisfied with my progress and ravenously hungry. It was three o'clock. I'd had that early-morning breakfast with Pete and a couple of slices of that killer banana bread. I weighed my options. Sparse leftovers from my refrigerator or the always-bounteous spread from Aunt Ibby's.

No contest. I headed downstairs.

CHAPTER 10

O'Ryan was already snarfing down chopped chicken livers from his own red bowl when I arrived. I'd taken the front stairs down to the first-floor foyer, which opens into Aunt Ibby's living room, while the cat had apparently scooted down the back stairs and through his cat door into her kitchen.

My aunt looked up from a paper-strewn table. "Hello, dear. Housework and homework all finished?"

"Done," I said. "I'm here to raid your refrigerator."

"*Mi* Frigidaire, *su* Frigidaire. Help yourself."

I opened the double-doored beauty and studied the orderly contents. "What's with all the paper? Working on the cookbook?"

When my previous year's class was studying the Trumbull family's history for the documentary production, Aunt Ibby had discovered Tabitha Trumbull's handwritten recipe collection in the vertical files at the library. She'd decided to transcribe, update and publish the *Tabitha Trumbull Cookbook,* to be used as a fund-raiser for the library's ongoing bookmobile project.

She waved a hand over the paper piles. "I know it looks disorganized," she said, "but it's really coming together quite nicely. I'm just trying to translate what 'a pinch of ginger' or 'a dab of butter' means to today's cook. By the way, how did you like the chocolate chip banana bread?"

"Divine. I had some for lunch. Saving the rest for Pete. Can I heat up this vegetable soup?"

"Sure. The mini chocolate chips were my idea. I don't think Tabitha would mind. Did you get a chance to talk to Pete about our little excursion this morning?"

"I did. I don't think he was too happy about it. He's sending somebody over to Goodwill to pick up the surveillance video and the Mickey Mouse remains." I popped the soup bowl into the microwave. "Pete doesn't seem to think that Stasia being there means anything."

"You know, Maralee, I've been thinking about that. Grace said the woman was looking for doll clothes. Remember I told you there's a box full of lovely handmade ones in the things I saved from the locker?"

I carefully moved aside a few of her papers and put the bowl of fragrant soup on the table. "I'd forgotten about that. How could she have known about them? That was one of the sealed boxes, wasn't it?"

My aunt nodded. "Uh-huh. It was just marked 'Dresses.' Think we should tell Pete about it?"

"I do. He said he'd come by later to talk to you about the van you saw—and the men who took our trash bags. This soup is fabulous. Tabitha's?"

"No. Mine. I didn't really get a good look at the van, you know. Or those men either. Didn't seem important. I thought it was the regular rubbish collection. Of course

O'Ryan knew better." The cat looked up at the sound of his name. "He could probably tell us the license plate number if he could talk."

The phone in my jeans pocket vibrated. The texted message was brief. "It's Pete. He wants to know if he can come over and talk to you now. Okay?"

"Certainly. Tell him to come right on over."

I did. And he did. Only about ten minutes had passed before O'Ryan ran into the foyer. I followed and together we watched from one of the tall, narrow windows flanking the front door as Pete pulled up, parked the Crown Vic and hurried up the steps. He paused on the landing, smiled and bent to tap the spot where the cat's pink nose pressed against the glass.

I pulled the door open and we shared a chaste front-door kiss, while O'Ryan wound himself around Pete's jean-clad ankles. "Come on out to the kitchen," I said. "Aunt Ibby's working on the cookbook."

"Hope I'm not interrupting genius at work." He followed me down the hall to the cozy room where my aunt had reduced the paper clutter to two neatly stacked piles. She'd also put away my soup bowl, started a fresh pot of coffee and placed a basket of blueberry muffins on the table. How does she do that stuff so fast?

"Hi, Ms. Russell," Pete said. "I understand that Nancy Drew here brought you along as sidekick on her little Goodwill caper this morning." Pete's compared me to that famous girl detective practically since the day we met. At first I'm sure he thought I was just nosy because I asked so many questions about police work. Later, when he found that I was really interested, he suggested the online criminology course. I was just beginning my second year. Pete was already in his fourth.

"A 'caper'? How exciting." My aunt beamed. "Sit down, Pete. Have a muffin. Maralee, pour Pete a cup of coffee, won't you, dear?"

Once we were all seated, Pete pulled the ever-present notebook and pencil from his jacket pocket. "What I'm here to ask you about mostly, Miss Russell, is that van you saw last night, and the men who took your trash bags."

"I don't know that I can tell you anything useful," she said. "I only went to the window because O'Ryan was making such a fuss. I do wish I'd paid more attention now, of course." She shrugged. "But I thought it was just the usual rubbish collection, I glanced out there, scolded the cat for waking me up, and went directly back to bed." O'Ryan looked up from his red bowl and gave her his I-told-you-so look.

"Just try your best." Pete's tone was gentle. "Can you describe the van for me?"

"Well, it was a big one. It had a door on the side. It had one in the back too."

"Were both doors open?"

"Why, yes. I think they were. And, Pete," she said, smiling, "both men were putting the bags into the van. One at each door. I remember that now."

"They must have been in a hurry," I said.

She nodded. "Didn't want anyone to notice. But O'Ryan noticed, didn't you, good boy?" The cat ignored the question and stalked from the room.

"Anything else?"

"They were each wearing big gloves. Like the regular rubbish men do."

Pete scribbled in his notebook. "What color was the van?"

"It was a light color, I'm sure. Maybe white or silver. It could even be pale blue. It's those new streetlights they put in. I know they save electricity, but they make the colors look strange. I'm sorry."

"That's okay," Pete said. "If I showed you some pictures of vans, could you tell me if any of them resemble the one you saw?"

"I'll try." She reached for the red-framed reading glasses lying on top of one of the paper piles.

He unfolded a sheet of color photos, showing side views of about a dozen vehicles and placed it in front of my aunt. She leaned closer. "It was shaped quite a bit like this one, but not so many windows." Pursing her lips, she moved her finger across the photos. "Ha! There it is. It looked like this one, only not red."

She'd selected a 2013 Chevy City Express cargo van. She shot Pete an inquiring look. "Does that make sense?"

"Sure does." He returned the sheet of photos to his pocket. "We've looked through that video you two thoughtfully asked Ms. Foster to save for us. Looks like we have a match."

"Same van?" I asked.

He handed me a grainy photo. "See what you think, Nancy."

It was a light-colored Chevy City Express cargo van, all right. "It's a 2012," I said. "But you nailed it, Aunt

Ibby." I squinted at the picture. "Could you make out the license plate, Pete?"

"The good news is we could. The bad news is it's a stolen vehicle."

"How about the men?" Aunt Ibby pushed the glasses down onto the end of her nose and peered over the top. "Any possible ID there?"

"No prints on anything so far, and they both wore those damned hoodies so the faces were mostly covered in the surveillance tape. But we got pretty good descriptions from the employees they'd talked to at the store." He reached for a second muffin. "These are good. Tabitha's?"

"No. Mine. Glad you like them."

"You think the trash stealers are involved in that man's murder, don't you?" I asked. "That's why you're spending time on it."

"You're right. That's why I want you two to stay out of it." Very grim cop face. "No more undercover work. Got it?"

Aunt Ibby and I nodded in unison and murmured promises to cease and desist meddling in police business. I meant it when I said I'd stop, but my aunt wasn't ready to give up.

"Pete," she said, "can you share the descriptions the employees gave of the men? Maybe if we have an idea of what they look like, we'd know whom we should avoid."

"Okay. That's reasonable. Here's what I have so far." He consulted the notebook. "One had dark hair and a beard. He's big. At least about six-three or more. The other one is shorter, five-ten. Blond. Clean-shaven. The blond one did most of the talking. The other one spoke with an accent. Ms. Foster said Polish or Russian. We have an artist working on sketches."

Aunt Ibby leaned back in her chair. "The matryoshkas. And the samovar."

Pete looked up. "What?"

"Russian," I said. "There were Russian things in the locker. You might want to check on Stasia too, the woman you said is harmless? River says she thinks she's some kind of a Russian princess or something."

Pete scribbled faster. After a moment he put his pencil and notebook on the table, not in his pocket, so I knew that more questions might be coming. I waited. Aunt Ibby was quiet. "You kept some of the Russian things, didn't you?"

"We did," my aunt said. "Some of them are still in the boxes. I can unpack them if you like, but the best one of all is right here in the dining room. Come on." She stood and motioned for us to follow.

The silver samovar sparkled, mirror bright, in the center of the long mahogany table. I could see the swirling colors and pinpoints of light before I'd even crossed the threshold of the room.

CHAPTER 11

Aunt Ibby's excited voice, chattering to Pete about Russian hallmarks and silver purity, seemed to come from a distance, like the teacher's voice in the Charlie Brown cartoons. I moved toward the samovar, grudgingly aware of both the beauty and the utility of the thing, while at the same time focusing my attention on the image beginning to take shape on one of its smooth, curving sides.

A row of people, six men, their backs to me, stood at the rail of a vessel. I could see the ocean stretching to the horizon—could almost feel the roll of the ship. That was all. In a blink the scene was gone. Pete's and Aunt Ibby's voices were again distinct. Neither of them had apparently noticed my momentary distraction.

As I turned away from the samovar, Aunt Ibby lifted it from the table, turning it over so that Pete could see the bottom. "See?" she said. "It has the Kokoshnik mark. Czar Nicholas II introduced it in 1896." I looked at where she pointed. A woman wearing a kerchief was pictured in an oval, along with some letters and numbers.

"Uh-huh." Pete didn't sound very interested. "Well, I need to get back to work. I've got the night off, after all. Lee, want to catch a movie or something?"

"Love to," I said. "Did you get around to talking to Scott Palmer? About the business card? You didn't tell us."

Change the subject. Don't think about the ship. Deal with it later.

"Yeah. I spoke to Palmer today," Pete said. "I had to ask him to come down to the station and talk to us about the . . . deceased."

I frowned. That didn't sound good. "Why did Scott have to go to the station? Couldn't you talk to him at WICH-TV?"

It seemed to take a long time for Pete to answer. "Chief Whaley had a few questions. They found Palmer's prints in that black Toyota."

"What does that mean?" Aunt Ibby asked. "Is Scott involved somehow in all this? The locker? The dead man? I don't understand."

I didn't understand either, but didn't say so. There was so darned much I didn't understand. I watched Pete's face.

"He says the man was an old reporter pal of his. Got into town a couple of days ago—been staying at Palmer's place. The car's a rental. Palmer admits he drove it a couple of times, showing his friend around Salem."

"Sounds reasonable," I said. "But why was Scott's friend following Aunt Ibby? Or do you think that could have been Scott?"

Pete shook his head. "Nope. Palmer was at the TV station all that morning. He's in the clear there. Chief wanted to get a look at the dead man's belongings. The stuff he left at Palmer's apartment."

"Scott agreed to that, didn't he?"

"Sure. Don't worry. Probably no problem there at all."

"*Probably?*" I didn't like the sound of that. I was about to ask what he meant when his phone buzzed and, frowning, he pulled it from his pocket. "Excuse me," he said. "Have to take this." He stepped back into the kitchen and returned just seconds later. "Have to get back to the station. Thanks for the coffee, Miss Russell. I'll let myself out." He started for the foyer, then turned back toward us. "Oh, Lee. You can stop calling the victim DG. They've released the name. Eric Dillon."

It had a vaguely familiar ring to it, but I was still puzzling over my vision of those men at the ship's rail and didn't give the name much thought. I said good-bye to Pete and waited until I heard the front door close. I was anxious to tell my aunt what I'd seen. Maybe she'd be able to make some sense of it.

"Aunt Ibby," I began, but she was already on her way out of the dining room.

"Come to the den with me, Maralee," she said, hurrying toward the room that houses a state-of-the-art computer and her many other electronic gadgets. "Eric Dillon! Imagine that! The papers will be full of that news, won't they?"

Dutifully I followed, searching my memory for a clue to the elusive name. The computer screen came to life, her fingers flew over the keys, as a tiny flash of recognition popped into my head. "Eric Dillon. A writer," I said. "Something about treasure hunting, wasn't it?"

"Right. *Lost and Found: Treasures of California*. Then

there was *Lost and Found: Treasures of the Florida Coast, Lost and Found: Treasures of the Pyramids* and a couple of similar ones. Makes me wonder what he was looking for in Salem."

"I wonder what he was looking for in Salem that got him killed," I said, "and mostly I wonder what *our* storage locker had to do with it."

"Look at this. His Facebook page says he's working on a new project—one that's taken years to research and has taken him all over America."

I looked over her shoulder. Dillon had posted a picture of a map of the United States. "Does he give a hint about the subject matter? Another treasure book?"

"I don't see anything else here about it. But look at this. Posted the day before yesterday." She pointed. "It's one of those selfie pictures you young folks like to take. It's him—and isn't that the Witch Museum in the background?"

The photo dispelled all doubts about the identity of the man in my vision. Eric Dillon was the dead man beside the little pine tree, and the man behind the wheel of the black Toyota. "It is," I said, "and that's Scott Palmer beside him."

She peered closely at the screen. "So it is. Pete told us Mr. Dillon was staying with Scott, and that Scott was showing his friend around Salem."

"That seems to back up Scott's story, doesn't it? What does the caption say?"

"'Met up with an old broadcast buddy. Showing me the sights around Salem, MA.'" There was a series of shots taken around the city—mostly of well-known tourist attractions, like the House of the Seven Gables, the Witch House, the Ropes Memorial Mansion. There was a picture of Scott standing in front of the WICH-TV building, shots of a couple of witch shops and one of a house I didn't recognize. There were no more selfies.

Aunt Ibby clicked on the house photo, enlarging it. "Know where that house is, Maralee?"

"No. Looks like a plain, old, everyday New England house to me." It was a three-story, peaked-roof, gray-clapboard house. Nothing looked special about it. "Where is it?"

"I'm pretty sure it's just a couple of streets away from here. Williams Street."

Williams is one of Salem's many one-way streets. It runs from the Common down to Bridge Street and isn't on any route I'd used in years. "Could be," I said.

"I think I'll take a walk over there." She clicked off the computer and stood, smoothing her skirt.

"What for?"

"Just curious. All his other photos are of famous places, popular shops. All, except this one. Maybe there's a historical plaque on it or something. Want to come with me?"

"I'd like to," I said, "but I still have work to do on my lesson plan. Think I'll go up to the study and see what titles we have on investigative reporting. By the way, do we have any Eric Dillon books up there?"

"Hmmm. Try nine thirteen point thirty-two," she said. "I'll be back soon." Not many home libraries have books filed according to the Dewey decimal system, but ours does.

"Let me know if you find anything interesting," I called as O'Ryan and I climbed the front staircase to the second-floor study. It may be my favorite place in the whole house. The walls are lined with books and my great-grandfather Forbes's huge desk is in the center of the room, his brass ship's clock on the wall. I bypassed the new computer perched incongruously on top of an old wooden card catalog cabinet and went directly to the nonfiction section my aunt had suggested. Not surprisingly, she'd been right. I pulled *Lost and Found: Treasures of the Florida Coast* from the shelf, sat in the comfortable leather swivel chair behind the desk, hoping to learn something about the sort of treasure Eric Dillon might be hunting in Salem. The cat curled up in a pretty patch of sun on the Oriental rug and closed his eyes.

The book, a fairly slim volume, was divided into ten sections, each one detailing somebody's lucky Florida find. The author, in his investigative reporter mode, had obviously done some serious research, tracking down original source materials, interviewing the searchers themselves for recent finds or close family descendants if the treasure was from long ago. Some accounts detailed prizes of enormous value, like Mel Fisher's 450-million-dollar cache of gold, silver and jewels from the Spanish galleon *Atocha*. Another told of a treasure fleet lost off the coast of Florida in a 1715 hurricane and of the hoard of gold and silver from that disastrous voyage, which a fortunate Florida family found in 2013.

I put the book down. Those men I'd seen on the samovar were surely aboard a ship. Not a Spanish galleon though. I closed my eyes and tried to visualize their clothes. Not ancient, but not modern either. I couldn't seem to focus my thoughts.

"Come on, O'Ryan," I said to the sleeping cat. "Let's go upstairs and try to bring back that scene in the bedroom mirror. It might be clearer there than it was in the doggoned fancy silver teakettle—kind of like a big-screen TV."

I couldn't figure out even the slightest connection between the dead writer, my poor ruined horse and the trash-stealing bandits. Maybe a little "gazing" would help somehow. I knew from past experience that I could often call up a vision if I wanted. The problem was, I hardly ever wanted to do so. The things were not fun for me. Never were. I'm sure some people think such a "gift" would be great to have. For me, mostly it hasn't been. What five-year-old kid would want to see her parents' deaths? Ever since this long-forgotten "gift" had recently returned, all it has ever brought me is scenes of death and dying.

I carried the Dillon book with me, planning to store it safely in the glass-fronted barrister's bookcase for a more careful reading later. With the cat following me, I returned to my apartment, passing through the kitchen, admiring the effect of my recent cleaning, and heading down the short hall to the living room.

"O'Ryan, you naughty boy," I scolded, spotting one of my bronzed pencil sharpeners on the floor. "You should be ashamed of yourself." The cat looked unconcerned as I replaced Lady Liberty in her accustomed spot for the second time that day.

CHAPTER 12

With the Dillon book safely stashed in the bookcase, I returned to the kitchen. O'Ryan stayed behind in the living room, choosing to sit in the zebra print wing chair, giving him a fine view of a pair of robins in the tree outside the bay window.

I was tempted to follow his lead, to sit in one of the Lucite chairs and look out the kitchen window, contemplating trees and birds. But that would be stalling, avoiding the tall, oval mirror and I knew it.

Shoulders squared, I marched into the bedroom, sat on the edge of my bed and faced the glass. "Okay, mirror," I said aloud, feeling quite like the Evil Queen, "show me what you've got."

The same shipboard picture popped right up, but this time it covered the whole surface of the mirror. The feeling of motion was more pronounced this time and I could see the rolling ocean waves clearly. The six men, as before, had their backs to me, but this time I could make out some details of their clothing. Four wore gray fedoras and the other two wore what I call "newsboy hats." Long-sleeved white shirts were topped by vests. I'd had enough experience with theater wardrobe to be pretty good with identifying period dress. I pegged these as early twentieth century, maybe around World War I.

I took a deep breath and whispered, "Would you turn around? Face me?"

That didn't work, but the scene changed. Just as the vision of the Toyota had expanded, like a camera moving back and widening the view, more of the ship showed. I could see other people lined up along the rail—men, women and even a few children, all in turn-of-the-century dress. In the far distance, beyond the waves, was a familiar outline. It was the Statue of Liberty.

No doubt about it. I was looking at people arriving in America over a century ago.

"But what does it mean? Who are you?" Frustration, almost to the point of tears, washed over me.

What good are visions when they don't make the least bit of sense?

I'm not proud of it, but I possess the legendary redhead's temper. Over the years I've learned to control it pretty well, but at that moment I wanted to kick that damned mirror across the room. Of course I didn't do it. Seven years' bad luck and all that. I stood up and gave it a rude push. "Go away," I said loudly. Just before the picture faded, one of the men turned, facing me, and smiled.

Even though the visions still rang no particular bells for me, O'Ryan's selection of which pencil sharpener to push onto the floor was beginning to reverberate.

Maybe Aunt Ibby could connect the dots better than
I was so far. She'd said she'd be right back and Williams
Street was only a couple of short blocks away. I decided
to wait for her in the backyard, where I could still catch
a few rays of late-summer sunshine. I sat in a weathered
Adirondack chair, head back, face upturned to the sun,
eyes closed, nearly dozing, when about twenty pounds
of yellow cat landed in my lap.

"Ooff," I grunted. "O'Ryan, give a little warning when
you're going to do that, will you?" I sat up straight, shov-
ing him off onto the ground, just in time to see the tail
end of a pink scooter passing by our back gate. Stasia?
Within a minute my aunt appeared, hurrying up the
driveway to where the cat and I waited.

"Hello, my dears," she said, slightly out of breath. She
bent to pat the cat, then sat in a chair matching mine.
"You should have come with me, Maralee. I've just had
a conversation with the most fascinating man!"

She had my full attention, thoughts of the bubble-
gum-chewing princess put aside for the moment.
"Really?" I smiled at her enthusiasm. "Glad to hear it.
The house didn't look all that interesting. Tell me about
this fascinating new man you've met."

She waved a dismissive hand in my direction, "He's
not *that* kind of fascinating, you silly goose. And the
house is absolutely worth more study. It seems to be
connected somehow to our storage locker—especially
to your carousel horse."

"No kidding? Now I wish I'd gone with you. Tell me
everything."

"Well, Mr. McKenna, that's the name of the man who
owns the house now, has lived in it since he was a little

boy. His family rented there back in the sixties and he says that I'm not the first person to ask questions about the place lately."

"Eric Dillon," I said, knowing I was right.

"Yep. He even had Mr. Dillon's business card."

"So, was Stasia over there asking questions too?"

"Stasia? The woman we saw at the auction?"

"Yes."

"Not that I know of, although I'm quite sure I saw her ride past me a little while ago on her motor scooter. An odd duck, isn't she?"

"She keeps showing up at the strangest times. Now tell me more about this mystery man who lives on Williams Street."

"Leonard. McKenna. He says that he remembers the old man who owned the house used to live up on the second floor. His family rented the first floor for years. His dad finally bought the place in the eighties."

"From the old man?"

"No. The old fellow was dead by then. They bought it from his son. But here's the thing. Mr. McKenna remembers that the old man was a really good wood-carver. He worked down at the Salem Willows. Kept the old merry-go-round up. Repaired the horses when they got broken or needed paint. Sometimes he made toys for the kids. Says his sister still has a matryoshka nest of dolls. His mother has some carved eggs. But listen to this." She leaned forward, eyes sparkling. "He says the old man had a carousel horse that he kept down in the basement. Used to let the little kids sit on it. He told them it used to be on a merry-go-round and that he was going to fix it up someday and put it back where it belonged."

"Wow," I said, wishing very much that I'd gone with her. "We need to tell Pete about this. I'll bet the police haven't made the connection between that house and my horse."

"I'll bet they haven't. And why would they? As you said, it's an ordinary New England house."

"I'm going to call Pete and tell him about it." I reached into my pocket for my phone. "Even though he made us promise not to meddle in police business."

She shrugged, smiling. "I didn't promise any such thing. I love meddling."

My call went to Pete's voice mail. Not unusual. I said, "Call me," and hung up. "What was the old man's name?" I asked my aunt.

"Mr. McKenna said everyone just called him 'Grandpa Nick,' but I'm sure it'll be easy enough to check real estate records from back then." A sly look crossed her face. "It's a matter of public record. Let's go for a little ride and see what we can find."

I knew we probably shouldn't do it—and I knew we would. "Okay," I said, "but first I need to tell you about something, I—um—saw."

"When you say it that way, it usually means you've had another vision." She reached for my hand. "Are you all right? Was it disturbing?"

"Not disturbing. More annoying, because it doesn't make any sense." I looked toward the back steps where O'Ryan sat, calmly grooming his long whiskers. "Although O'Ryan seems to have figured some of it out." I described the scene I'd viewed in the samovar that morning, and the expanded view the bedroom mirror had offered, including the famous statue in the distance. "That smarty-pants cat has knocked the Statue of Liberty pencil sharpener off my bookcase twice today."

"It looks as though the people on your boat are coming to America, approaching New York—Ellis Island, I imagine—sometime in the early 1900s," she said.

"I get that part, but why would I care about these people? And what does that have to do with a carousel horse? Or a dead writer? Or me?"

"Maybe the Williams Street house is a connection," she said. "At least to the dead writer And maybe the carousel horse. Ready to go to the registry of deeds? Have you finished your housework?"

"I have some laundry to throw into the machine," I said, heading for the back door. "I'll be back here in a couple of minutes."

Although I have my own space on the third floor, my aunt and I still share the big first-floor laundry room, with its almost brand-new washer and dryer.

I tossed a few pairs of jeans and a half-dozen dark-colored tops, along with a denim vest, into a bag and hurried back downstairs. Aunt Ibby was already in the laundry room busy folding sheets. I paused in my prespotting procedure—a mustard stain on my green Boston Celtics T-shirt—to watch her fold a queen-sized fitted sheet into a neat square. I've been watching her do that ever since I was little and I still can't do it. After a couple of deftly smoothed pillowcases were added to her pile, she shook the wrinkles from a multi-colored quilt.

"Here, take the other end and help me with this, will you, Maralee? It's quite heavy." We faced one another. I held one corner of the quilt in each hand and she did the same.

"This is lovely. Is it new?"

"Can't identify it, can you?" She smiled. "I barely recognized it myself, after I'd run it through the washer a couple of times. It's what they call a 'crazy quilt.' See how the patches are all different sizes and shapes? Thrifty, old New Englanders liked to use up every little scrap of fabric. The colors are as vibrant as new. I'm going to use it on my bed."

We moved toward one another, then back, in the peculiar do-si-do motion quilt folding involves. Recognition dawned.

"It's the quilt my horse was wrapped in. That dirty, old quilt. I would have thrown it away. I can't believe it's the same one."

"I know. I'm awfully pleased. It's a beautiful piece. I think I like this even better than the samovar." Folding completed, she lifted the quilt with both arms, placing it on the table. "I think it's all handmade," she said, stroking the top of the varicolored fabric.

O'Ryan leaped up onto the table, walked gingerly around the sheet and pillowcase pile. He put one paw on the edge of the neatly folded quilt, sniffing at the edges. He turned unblinking golden eyes on me, then climbed into the center of Aunt Ibby's new bedcovering, turned around a couple of times, lay down and closed his eyes.

"Get down from there, you naughty boy," I scolded. The cat, unmoving, didn't even open his eyes.

"Oh, let him be," my aunt said. "He looks so comfortable. He won't hurt it, will you, boy? Let's get going. We want to get over there before the registry closes."

"Can't you do it online?"

"Already tried that. The deed we're looking for is too old." She sounded pleased. "This'll be hands-on research. It's what I do."

"Okay. Let's go. My car or yours?"

We decided on the Buick. The registry of deeds is on Congress Street, a straight shot from the Common, past the Hawthorne Hotel, across Derby Street south. We found a visitor's parking spot easily and made our way past a confusing warren of offices and arrived at our destination by three o'clock.

"They're open until four-thirty," my aunt said. "That should give us plenty of time to find what we need."

By this time I wasn't exactly sure what that might be, but had every confidence that Aunt Ibby knew what she was doing. The clerk behind the counter was a library friend, anxious to help with research. Not knowing last names or exact dates would present a problem to most people, but it was a piece of cake to an experienced reference librarian.

Within half an hour we had a photocopy of a 1936 deed to the Williams Street house. It was made out in the names of Nikita and Lydia Novikova.

So I had the name of the man who'd carved my horse. It had to be more than coincidence that Novikova was also the last name of the scooter-riding, bubble-blowing Stasia.

We were about to leave the office when I paused at the doorway and turned back toward the counter. "Excuse me," I said to the clerk, "but has anybody else asked about this deed recently?"

"Don't know. Let me check the log." He watched his computer screen for a moment. "Interesting. Yes. A fellow doing historical research picked up a copy of it a couple of days ago."

CHAPTER 13

"So," my aunt said as we returned to the parking lot, "now we have a name. Nikita Novikova."

"Grandpa Nick," I said. "I'm thinking that the Novikovas are on that ship I saw arriving in America."

"I think so too. Now the serious research begins." She'd put on her wise-old-owl face.

"We're meddling."

"I know." She smiled. "I love meddling."

We climbed into the Buick and headed for home. It was a quiet ride. Ideas swirled in my head. Probably in Aunt Ibby's too. We pulled into the garage and walked together toward the house. O'Ryan waited on the back steps.

"Want to come in and compare notes?" she asked.

I glanced at my watch. "I've got to put away my schoolwork and change my clothes," I said. "Pete'll be here at six-thirty. We're going to a movie."

"That's nice, dear. I have book club this evening, but first I'm going straight to my computer and see what I can dig up on Nikita and Lydia."

"On a first-name basis already, I see."

"Might as well be. I intend to poke around in their lives as much as I possibly can."

"Good luck," I said. "I'll check back with you later." She went into her kitchen and I opened the door to the stairway leading up to my apartment. O'Ryan looked back and forth between us for a moment, then—via the cat door—followed my aunt.

I entered my living room and glanced around, once again visualizing my restored carousel horse in the bay window. I hurried to my bedroom, changed into white jeans—it wasn't Labor Day yet—and a navy turtleneck. I began to organize the mess I'd made on the kitchen counter. I closed the laptop, put it away and gathered the books into a neat pile. I noticed a brand-new package of blank index cards among the notebooks and legal pads. I'd always used the handy, little lined surfaces for schoolwork—both as student and teacher—but I'd learned fairly recently that index cards are an awfully good tool for organizing random bits of information when one is trying to find answers to a tangled string of questions. I peeled the cellophane away and put the stack of cards in a space I'd cleared on the counter.

Selecting a card and a nice sharp number-two pencil, I wrote, *Nikita Novikova lived in the Williams Street house.* On the next card I wrote, *Why did somebody kill Eric Dillon?* Next came: *What is somebody looking for that was in our locker?* I was scribbling faster with each card. *Who are the men who stole our trash? How is Stasia involved?*

I spread the cards on a corner of the counter and stared at them. Moved them around a little. Stared some more. All questions. No answers. No bolt of lightning. No lightbulb over my head.

The cuckoo clock announced six o'clock. She'd barely finished her sixth coo-coo when I heard the Winter Street door chimes ring out "The Impossible Dream." Pete must be early. I started down the stairs, and had almost reached the foyer when Aunt Ibby approached from her living room. She'd changed her clothes for the book club meeting and looked elegant in a light wool gray dress and gray suede high heels.

"Must be Pete," she called. "I'll get it." The doorbell chimed again. As she reached for the alarm system pad, O'Ryan streaked past me and planted himself firmly, back arched and teeth bared, between her and the door.

"It's not Pete," I called, dashing down the last two steps. "Don't open it. Look at the cat."

She pulled her hand away from the knob and backed away from the door. "Who is it, Maralee?" she whispered. "What should we do?"

I walked carefully behind the cat and peeked out the side window. "Who is it?"

"It's Scott Palmer, Lee," came the reply. "May I come in for a minute, please?"

I hadn't seen Scott for over a year, although I watched his newscasts on WICH-TV fairly often.

"Just a minute, Scott," I said, bending to pick up the cat. He was no longer snarling, but still stood between Aunt Ibby and the door. "It's okay, boy," I told him. "See? It's just Scott." I held him up to the window. "You remember Scott, don't you?"

The big cat squirmed and jumped down to the floor, then slowly backed away, watching as I opened the door.

"Hi, Scott," I said. "Come in. You remember my aunt?"

"Yes, of course. Hello, Miss Russell. See you still have Ariel's cat." He turned to face me. "Is there somewhere I can talk to you privately for a minute, Lee?"

No way was I about to invite him up to my apartment. My previous experience with Scott hadn't been entirely pleasant. He was good-looking in a rugged-jock sort of way, but I didn't trust him. "I think so. May we use your living room for a few minutes, Aunt Ibby?"

She nodded. "Certainly, dear. Stay as long as you like. I'm off to my meeting. Nice to see you again, Scott." She spoke a hushed "Here, kitty, kitty" to O'Ryan, who dutifully followed her from the hall without a backward glance in my direction.

Scott followed me into the living room and sat gingerly on a pine tavern chair.

"What's going on, Scott? What do you want to talk to me about?"

"Are you still dating that detective? Mondello?"

"Yes. Why?"

"He and Chief Whaley made me go down to the police station . . . asked me a lot of questions about Eric Dillon's murder. You know about that, don't you?"

"Yes, of course."

"They sound as though they think I had something to do with it." He looked down at his hands for a moment. "Jeez, Lee. Eric was an old friend. I liked him. Why would I want him dead?"

I didn't have an answer for that, so I didn't say anything.

"I need to know. Has Mondello told you anything

about why they're doing this to me? Do they really think I've done . . . something?"

"Pete doesn't discuss police business with me, Scott. But I'm sure you have nothing to worry about. Just answer their questions the best you can." I hoped I sounded encouraging. "I'm sure it'll be fine. Just tell them the truth."

"There's this one thing," he said. "Eric told me something in strictest confidence. That's what he called it. 'In strictest confidence.' It's about what he was looking for in Salem. He said I wasn't to tell anybody, at least until after the book comes out."

"That's a confidence you definitely can't keep," I said. "You have to call Pete and tell him everything. This isn't about a book. It's about your friend's murder. You have to tell the police."

He was quiet for a long moment, then looked up and smiled. "Well, thanks, Lee. You've been a big help. I'll remember what you said." He stood. "This was really helpful."

"So you'll call Pete?"

"Oh, sure."

We were about to step into the foyer when O'Ryan raced past us and put his front paws up on the windowsill, his nose against the glass. I looked at my watch. Six-thirty on the dot.

"That'll be Pete now." I opened the door, just as Pete's Crown Vic rolled to a stop at the curb right behind Scott's yellow Jeep.

They passed one another on the front steps. Scott bobbed his head. "Detective."

Pete looked up at me and raised an eyebrow. He nodded in Scott's direction. "Palmer."

Pete came inside and I closed the door. "What's going on? They trying to hire you back at the TV station?"

I laughed. "Nope. I'm afraid my late-show psychic days are well behind me. Come on upstairs and I'll tell you all about it."

Once inside my kitchen we shared a delicious kiss, which could have easily led to more kisses if I hadn't had so much to tell him about what Aunt Ibby and I had learned, as well as what Scott had told me. "I've had a very busy day," I began. "I mean, Aunt Ibby and I have had a busy day."

Pete smiled and sat on one of the tall stools beside the counter, right in front of the index cards I'd so recently and so fruitlessly spread out there. "So, what have the Snoop Sisters been up to?"

I sat beside him, took a deep breath, preparing to begin my story, when Pete picked up an index card. "What's this?" He picked up the card about Nikita Novikova and the Williams Street house. "How'd you know about the house on Williams Street?"

"Aunt Ibby saw it on Eric Dillon's Facebook page, so she went over there to take a look at it."

Pete put one hand on his forehead. "You mean I had one officer driving up and down streets most of the day looking for that house, and another one searching Google Earth for it, and you knew where it was all along?"

"Aunt Ibby did. It's only a couple of streets over from here, you know."

"I know that now. She went over there?"

"She did, and she talked to the man who lives there. A Mr. McKenna. He's lived there most of his life."

"Your aunt is way ahead of us on this. We just got his name about an hour ago. Chief's sending somebody over in the morning to talk to him, see if he knows anything about Dillon taking a picture of his house."

"He does. Apparently, he talked to Dillon too. Aunt Ibby said Mr. McKenna has his business card. Besides that, he remembers an old man who lived upstairs and kept a carousel horse in the basement."

I definitely had his full attention. He put the card down. "Dillon knew about the house. And he must have known about the horse too, if he spoke with McKenna. Is your aunt at home now? I need to know more about this."

I shook my head. "No. Sorry. She's gone to her book club meeting."

I told him everything I could remember. I told him that the old man had carved toys for the neighborhood kids, and how Mr. McKenna's father had bought the house from the old man's son.

"And you got Novikova's name too. How'd you get that?"

I shrugged and tried to look modest. "Registry of Deeds."

"Did I ever tell you you'd make a good cop?"

I laughed. "Several times. But seriously, Pete, Stasia's last name is Novikova too. And she's interested in doll clothes. We have a whole box full of doll clothes that was in the locker. That can't be coincidence."

"No, it can't. We'll talk to her. Want to tell me what

Palmer was here for? If it's none of my business, you can say so."

"Oh, it absolutely is your business. He wanted to know if you'd told me anything about why you and Chief Whaley were questioning him about Eric Dillon's murder. He sounded really upset about it."

"What did you tell him?"

"That you don't discuss police business with me and that he should just answer the questions and tell the truth."

"Good."

"There's more. He said that Eric had told him something in confidence about what he was looking for in Salem. That he'd made Scott promise not to tell anyone until after the book came out. I told him he has to call you, to tell you everything."

"Did he agree?"

I leaned forward, putting both elbows on the counter. "I don't know. That's the thing about Scott. You never know if you're getting a straight answer. He said 'sure,' but I don't know."

"Don't worry about it. You did fine. Come on. Smile."

I attempted a smile, but didn't quite pull it off. "There's more," I said.

Pete knew me pretty well. His expression turned serious and he put a comforting arm across my shoulders. "You've been seeing things again. Want to tell me about it?"

So I did. "Does that mean anything to you?" I asked. "Aunt Ibby and I are thinking I might be seeing the Novikovas coming to America."

"It could be," he said. "It just could be. Remember I

told you the murder weapon was probably a garrote of some kind?"

"Uh-huh."

"I was right. It'll be in the papers tomorrow, so there's no harm in telling you. The forensics guys said it was a garrote made of leather, but here's the strange thing. They say there are small, flat triangular pieces of metal on it. Dillon was strangled, and the metal things stuck in his throat."

"That would account for the ribbon of blood I saw— we saw. Interesting. And very, very weird."

"Chief thought so too. Did I ever tell you about his old newspaper-clipping file?"

He hadn't. We don't talk about Chief Whaley much. "Newspaper clippings?"

"Right. It's a big, thick, old-fashioned file envelope. Clippings about crimes from all the way back to the fifties. Maybe older. Anyway, the garrote reminded him of something he'd read a long time ago."

I sat up straight, facing him. "What was it?"

"A murder in Connecticut. Happened in the seventies. An old guy, a baker, was strangled with a weapon just like that. A thick leather thong with triangular metal pieces embedded in it. They found the poor old man dead in his own bakery, the murder weapon still on the body."

"Did they catch the killer?"

"No. Never did, but here's the thing. The man's name was Alex Chopiak. The clipping said he'd come to America from Russia in 1915 and opened his bakery. He always told people he'd been a chief baker in the court of Czar Nicholas II. Funny thing though. Nothing was stolen. There was money in the cash register. The only thing disturbed was a big papier-mâché display wedding cake. Smashed to smithereens."

"They say that Stasia thinks she's Grand Duchess Anastasia, the czar's daughter."

"I know. We'll talk to her again. Don't expect to get much though. She's kind of . . . vague."

"So the murder weapon from the baker's murder still exists?"

"A photo of it anyway. The people in the Russian community back then blamed Chopiak's death on a witch."

"Sure. When in doubt, blame a witch. We'll have to talk to River about that. But, Pete, are you thinking that maybe two of the men in my vision could be Chopiak and Novikova, arriving in America in 1915?"

"Seems possible."

"You can't tell the chief about my vision though." Chief Whaley and I have a history. I'm not one of his favorite people. He wouldn't be at all pleased to learn that his lead detective had a nosy scryer for a girlfriend.

"Sure can't tell him anything about that."

"What are you going to do?"

He stood, pulled me to my feet, kissed me and said, "I'm going to take my woman to the movies. Let's get out of here before that damned bird crows again."

CHAPTER 14

"It's such a nice night. Want to walk?" Pete asked. "We can talk some more on the way."

"Sure. If we hurry we can still make the seven o'clock." Cinema Salem is within easy walking distance of Winter Street, and he was right about it being a nice night. I pulled on a lightweight red jacket and we left the house via the back door. The sun was low in the sky and clouds were streaked with pink. The temperature had dropped several degrees and the leaves on a few of the trees on the Common had already begun to turn to a reddish gold. "Might as well enjoy what's left of summer. Winter's coming."

We walked briskly, crossing Williams Street on our way. Pete paused for a second on the corner and looked at the sign. "Practically next door," he said, shaking his head. "Did the man who lives there now know anything else about the Novikovas?"

We kept walking, passing the statue of Roger Conant and the Witch Museum. "He didn't really remember much. It was a long time ago and he was a young kid.

Just an old man they called Grandpa Nick, who worked at the Salem Willows amusement park, where he repaired the flying horses. He used to carve toys for the neighborhood kids. He had that wooden horse in the cellar and said he was going to fix it up someday and put it back where it belonged."

"Nick. Nikita. The pieces are starting to fit together."

"Some of them are. But quite a few of the pieces lead straight to our locker—and to us. To Aunt Ibby and me."

"We're on it, babe. You know I can't tell you everything, but we're on it. Don't worry."

It was just seven when we arrived at the box office. Cinema Salem is not your state-of-the-art multiplex with reclining seats and all the first-run movies. It's an independent neighborhood theater, kind of old and kind of small, but it's become one of our favorite date-night venues. Besides, they have great popcorn, loaded with real butter. There's usually at least one new movie, along with some old classics, some foreign films, some local indie productions and kid flicks. Pete and I hardly ever want to see the same one, so we always toss a coin to see who picks.

"Easy choice for me," Pete said. "The new Bond movie is finally here. 007 for me. What's yours?"

I pointed to a colorful poster displayed behind glass. "My favorite foreign film of all time!" I was delighted. "It's Chinese. *Raise the Red Lantern*. I cry every time I see it."

Pete groaned. "Chinese. With subtitles. Oh, boy. I'll cry if you win this time."

"Hate to see a grown man cry," I said. I called "heads" and tossed the quarter.

"Tails. You lose!" His glee was undisguised. We got a big bucket of that to-die-for popcorn and prepared to watch James Bond's latest caper.

"I have to admit it. I really enjoyed seeing Bond," I said. "Anyway, I have *Raise the Red Lantern* at home on DVD." It was dark when we left the theater and there was a real chill in the air. We walked quickly past St. Peter's Church and started down Brown Street.

"Glad you liked it. It's not even ten o'clock yet. Want to go anyplace else?"

"Not really. Let's go home and I'll make you hot chocolate with Marshmallow Fluff on top and a slice of chocolate chip banana bread."

"Sounds like a plan." He took my hand. We passed the Witch Museum, which is really spooky-looking at night, and stopped at the curb on the corner of Williams Street. "Want to take a short detour?" he asked. "I'd like to take a look at that house."

"Good idea. I would too."

The house wasn't far from the corner. There was a street lamp right in front of it, so it stood out from its neighbors on either side. We looked at it from across the street. "Pretty ordinary-looking, isn't it?" Pete said. "In fact, it looks like about half the houses in Salem. No wonder my people took so long to identify it. Just a plain-Jane, old house."

For some reason I felt as though I should defend it. "It's nice and neat though. Looks like fresh paint and the window boxes are pretty."

"That's not what I meant." Pete gave my hand a

squeeze. "Your aunt was pretty sharp to notice it on Dillon's Facebook page. It was the ordinariness that made it stand out to her from the other pictures. Want to go across the street and take a closer look?"

"Might as well." The fire pit in the side yard hadn't been visible from our vantage point on the opposite side of the street. It was a cozy sight. A group of people were gathered around the glowing coals and the sound of laughter drifted toward us. I felt as though we were intruding and gave Pete's hand a tug. "Let's go," I whispered.

"Right," he whispered back, dropping my hand. With my back to the house, and with Pete behind me, I started toward the other side of the street—and directly into the path of a man carrying a pizza box. That is, he *was* carrying a pizza box—until I collided with him and sent the box flying onto a nearby hedge.

"Oh, I'm so sorry, sir," I said. "Are you all right?"

The man laughed. "No harm done, miss. My fault. I should watch where I'm going." He retrieved the pizza box, still miraculously right side up, from the top of the hedge, then pointed to the group in the yard. "That bunch of gannets over there say they're still hungry. After hot dogs and hamburgers and gallons of soda, they sent me out for pizza!" He cocked his head to one side. "Nice night for a walk. You two from the neighborhood?"

"Winter Street," I said. "I'm Lee Barrett and this is Pete Mondello."

"Pleased to meet you both." He offered his free hand, first to Pete, then to me. "Leonard McKenna."

"How do you do, Mr. McKenna?" I grasped his hand.

"I think you met my aunt Isobel Russell earlier today. I'm happy to meet you, but we're keeping you from your guests. Mustn't let that pizza get cold."

"Miss Russell. Yes. Charming woman. Real interested in my house." He pushed a low wooden gate open. "Come on in for a minute, meet the family, have some s'mores—if they haven't eaten them all."

I began to say, "Oh, we couldn't . . . ," but Pete took my elbow, steering me toward the gate.

"Can't ever turn down s'mores," he said. "Thanks."

There were two women and two men seated beside the fire pit. The two men stood when we approached, and I saw that they were young. Teenagers, I thought. Very tall, very polite teenagers.

Leonard McKenna handed the pizza to one of the women. "Here you go, sis. Look, I found these neighbors wandering around, so I brought them along." He launched into introductions. The women were his sister and his mother. The boys were nephews. "This is Ms. Barrett and Mr. Mondello. From over on Winter Street. Kids, go get a couple more chairs."

So Pete and I joined that friendly circle of neighbors. We each declined the offer of pizza, but happily nibbled on s'mores and learned some things I could hardly wait to note on my index cards. Pete identified himself right away as a detective, but he didn't really have to. One of the boys, Colin, played hockey at the same rink where Pete coached a peewee team and had recognized him right away.

"You working on the case about that guy who took a picture of this house, Coach?"

"I am," Pete admitted, holding up his right hand. "But, honest, I came for the s'mores, not to ask questions."

"Wish I'd taken the time to talk to that poor soul," Mr. McKenna said, "but I had to get to work. He gave me his card, you know, and asked me to call him later. He wanted to talk about the house, I guess."

"That was too bad," Mrs. McKenna spoke up. "We don't mind talking about the house at all. I remember Old Man Novikova well. His wife too. Real nice folks. He used to make toys for my kids, Lennie and Colleen both. After he died, Lydia—that's his wife—gave me one of those nested things. You know, you open it and there's another one inside it?"

I nodded. "A matryoshka doll."

"No. Colleen has one of those." She gestured toward her daughter. "Mine is different. Not dolls. Lydia gave it to me after Grandpa Nick passed. Mine is an Easter egg with more Easter eggs inside. They get smaller and smaller."

"I'll bet it's beautiful," I said.

"It's real pretty. Want to see it?"

"We don't want to bother you—" Pete began, but I interrupted.

"I'd love to see it," I said, "if it's not too much trouble."

Pete raised an eyebrow, but didn't comment.

"No problem," said Mrs. McKenna. "Kevin, run inside and get my egg." The boy stood and headed for the back door of the house. "He knows just where it is. I keep it in a special plastic case right on my dining-room side-board. Been there since she gave it to me."

The woman called Colleen smiled. "We always wanted to play with it when we were kids. She never let us though.

That Lydia was so nice before she got sick. A wonderful seamstress. She gave me a gorgeous embroidered table-cloth. I only use it at Christmas and Thanksgiving."

Colleen's words made me think of the delicate stiches, the careful color coordination evident in Aunt Ibby's quilt. "My aunt has a patchwork quilt that might be something Lydia made," I said.

Mr. McKenna handed his sister a slice of pizza, then turned toward me. "Your aunt told me about the storage locker auction and the carousel horse," he said. "It's got to be the same one that used to be in our cellar when I was a kid. The old man used to love that horse. He told us we could tell it all our secrets—that it would never tell anyone. Said it was the best 'secret keeper' in the world. We used to think it was like going to confession! I whispered into those wooden ears all the time. Hey, I'll just bet that old Lydia made that quilt. Can't all be a big coincidence, can it?"

"I don't believe in coincidences," Pete said. He was smiling, but his cop voice was back.

I snapped a few cell phone pictures of Mrs. McKenna's egg to show to Aunt Ibby and asked her whether the family had ever met Stasia.

"Oh, my . . . yes," she said. "I remember the first time I saw Stasia. She came here from Colorado several times to spend the summers with her grandparents. Cute, little thing. Smart as a whip. Of course she's changed a lot since then." She shrugged her shoulders and added, "She and Colleen were kind of pen pals for a long time. They were around the same age. The letters stopped coming after a while though. Next time we saw Stasia was at Lydia's funeral. She was . . . different by then. Pretended she didn't even know us."

It was nearly eleven when we left the McKennas' backyard and walked toward Winter Street. I was surprised by the amount of information we'd gathered about the house on Williams Street, and maybe Pete had picked up something useful to help with the Dillon investigation. It was hard to tell.

Pete and I cut through Oliver Street to our backyard. "That was interesting, about Stasia," I said. "Are you going to talk to her about our trash?"

"We'll get to that. First things first. I have a murder investigation to run."

Of course he was right. I tend to get bogged down in details, I guess. Trivia like doll dresses and embroidered tablecloths and painted horses, instead of concentrating on stolen cars and leather garrotes and the dead man.

Two dead men, if you count the baker from Connecticut.

CHAPTER 15

We decided against the hot chocolate and banana bread idea. We'd both eaten enough s'mores to last us until next summer, and Pete needed to go home and get some sleep. I didn't mention it to him, but I was anxious to get back to filling out index cards. Our un-planned stop on Williams Street had yielded a wealth of information about the Novikovas. Besides that, I wanted to write down what Scott had told me, along with Pete's story about Chief Whaley's newspaper-clipping collec-tion before I forgot any of it.

Pete walked with me to the Winter Street door, kissed me good night and left for his own apartment. Once inside the front hall, where O'Ryan waited, I peeked into Aunt Ibby's living room. All was dark and quiet—and it was late, so I assumed she'd gone to bed—and with the cat following, I climbed the stairs.

The papers and books and index cards were still spread out on the counter. I carried the books and legal pad into my bedroom and, avoiding looking directly at the mirror, stashed them in my antique writing desk.

I hurried back to the kitchen—and the waiting stack of fresh index cards. I kicked off my shoes and began scribbling:

> *The carousel horse was in the cellar of the Williams Street house when Mr. McKenna was a little kid back in the sixties.*
>
> *Colleen McKenna and Stasia were friends.*
>
> *Scott Palmer was friends with Dillon and is keeping his secrets.*
>
> *Nikita Novikova's wife was named Lydia. (Did she make the quilt?)*
>
> *Chief Whaley's clipping file: There was a similar murder to Dillon's in Connecticut in the 1970s.*
>
> *Connecticut murder victim was a Russian baker who said he worked in the czar's court. Baker came to America in 1915.*
>
> *Did Nikita and the baker come to America together in 1915 on the ship I saw?*
>
> *The murder weapon—A leather garrote with metal triangles in it.*
>
> *The Russians in Connecticut blamed witches. (Ask River why.)*

I put all the cards, the new ones and the ones I'd written earlier, into a neat pile.

Now what? I have a stack of questions without answers.

I picked up the cards and absentmindedly began shuffling them, the same way I'd shuffled the tarot cards.

Maybe if I lay them down in some sort of pattern like River does, I thought, *they'll begin to make sense.*

Feeling a little silly, and glad no one was watching

except the cat, I carried the stack of cards over to the kitchen table. Sitting down, I slowly lifted the top card, turned it face up and placed it in the center of the glass.

Why did somebody kill Eric Dillon?

Interesting. That was, after all, the main question. I lifted the next card, turned it over and put it above the first one.

What is somebody looking for that was in our locker?

I turned over the next two. Both showed the same name.

Colleen and Stasia were friends.

How is Stasia involved?

Coincidence? What was it Pete had said just about an hour ago? "I don't believe in coincidences," he'd told Leonard. I decided right then that I didn't either. I gathered up all cards on the table, grabbed a rubber band from my junk drawer, secured the stack and put it, along with a couple of blank index cards, into my purse. Tomorrow I'd go over to the Common and look for Stasia. Nobody, including Pete and Aunt Ibby, seemed to believe the eccentric woman could contribute anything helpful. "Just a local character," they'd called her. Yet, Stasia continued to show up in places that related to our locker, and the items we'd found there.

She knows something we don't know. No coincidence there at all, I thought.

"What do you think about that, cat?" I asked O'Ryan, who was once again stretched out along the windowsill like a long, furry draft protector. "I'm going to interview the local crazy lady. Maybe get my palm read in the process."

O'Ryan gave a cat equivalent of a shoulder shrug, hopped down from his perch and strolled toward the bedroom. He was right. It was definitely bedtime. Cuckoo agreed and announced midnight.

I changed into pajamas and climbed into bed. But sleep didn't come easily. I lay awake for a long time, something elusive nibbling at my brain. I mentally ran through the index cards, and through the day's events. What was I missing? Was there an important clue I'd overlooked? I couldn't help thinking about the things Aunt Ibby and I had learned in the short time since we'd bought the locker. Things. Maybe I should compose a card about the actual things involved so far. *Samovar. Horse. Mickey Mouse. Black Toyota. Ship. Garrote. Doll dresses . . .*

It had the same effect as counting sheep. I knew there were more, but I felt myself drifting off to sleep, the brain-nibbling missing clue still missing.

In the morning I padded out into the kitchen, turned on the TV, then headed straight for the window and closed it. Somehow, during the night, summer had gone away and fall had arrived in New England, complete with a chill wind and, according to WICH-TV's Wanda the Weathergirl, reports of snow flurries in the White Mountains. I was anxious to watch the morning news, hoping I'd learn some more about the dead Eric Dillon and the break-in at Carbone's.

Considering that the previous evening's fare had consisted mainly of heavily buttered popcorn and sugary, gooey s'mores, I decided that a reasonably healthful breakfast might be in order. Though I'm admittedly no cook, I can scramble eggs, make toast and pour orange juice. I watched the screen while I assembled the ingredients on the counter. Phil Archer, who used to be the night anchor at the station, had been relegated to morning show host duties. He read a few commercials, announced the score of the Red Sox–Royals game and ran a brief video of the opening of a new Nordstrom store.

"Come on, Phil," I mumbled. "Get to the real news, will you?" O'Ryan climbed up onto a stool and made a few kittenish swipes at my egg. I rescued it before it could roll off the edge, then reached for the large-sized box of his favorite morning kitty kibble. "Keep your paws off my breakfast, cat. I haven't forgotten yours." I turned my back to the screen while I filled O'Ryan's bowl and almost missed the shot of Scott Palmer standing in front of Carbone's shop.

It was hard to believe that the station would assign Scott to cover an event he might possibly be involved in. It occurred to me almost immediately that Scott, being Scott, probably hadn't told the station's management that he *was* involved.

The report was pretty forthright and didn't tell me anything I hadn't already heard from Pete. There was an artist's sketch of what the forensics people had determined the murder weapon might look like. Scott didn't point out the triangular metal pieces, but the sketch showed them clearly. He didn't mention what assignment Eric Dillon had been pursuing in Salem either, nor what business he had in the vicinity of Carbone's shop. I guessed that the police had limited the information the station could release. The part that interested me most was an interior shot of the inside of the shop.

Obviously filmed from outside the open doorway—
yellow crime-scene tape visible at the edges of the
frame—the camera panned around the large room.
The Peter Hunt–style table looked just as it had when
Pete and I were there, ditto the Victorian chairs. But
spread out in the center of the room was what was left
of my poor horse.

I put two slices of whole wheat bread into the toaster
and moved closer to the screen. The camera had
zoomed in on the horse parts. It occurred to me that
maybe the carnage wasn't as bad as I'd first thought.
The four legs were lined up in a row, and the hindquar-
ters were in two equal pieces above the legs. The head
section was pretty scary-looking, leaning against the base
of Paul's workbench, and I could see where the jewels
had been pried out. The carved rose dangled forlornly
at an awkward angle.

The camera lingered the longest on the body section,
which was clearly hollow inside. The camera panned the
parts as Phil Archer intoned, "Police speculate that the
intruders may have suspected that something of value
was hidden within this old carousel horse. It has not yet
been determined whether or not the murder of investigative reporter Eric Dillon, whose body was discovered
within the warehouse property, is connected to the
break-in at the Carbone studio."

"You can't be serious," I told the screen as I scram-
bled my egg harder than necessary. "Of course they're
connected. Don't you think Eric Dillon was interested
in the horse too?"

Naturally, Phil didn't answer my question. I listened
as Scott wound up the segment. "Chief Whaley has

announced that he'll make a further announcement about the Dillon murder at noon today. WICH-TV will bring it to you live."

I poured the orange juice, carried the reasonably healthy breakfast to the table and turned off the TV. Phil Archer's words about Eric Dillon lingered in my mind. Not so much about Dillon's connection to the break-in, but that Phil had referred to him as an investigative reporter. In the next room I had a desk full of books on the subject, and in a couple of weeks I'd have a class full of students wanting to learn what I knew about the job. It was about time I put my book smarts to use and got into the field myself. That would give the Tabby's investigative reporting 101 class some real-time relevance and, with a little bit of luck, would give me some answers. I'd start today with a walk over to the Salem Common, and maybe an interview with the palm-reading Stasia Novikova.

I remembered some of the things I'd read for my class preparation about interviewing. I'd underlined quite a few passages in the Barbara Walters book and the important thing I carried away was Barbara's philosophy about how people need to be treated. She wrote that it was her responsibility to make people comfortable, that the interviewer needs to make them feel good about themselves, to keep their dignity.

There's no arguing with success like Barbara's. I can do that.

I thought then about how the people I knew thought about Stasia. River said she's a "local character." Pete told me he doesn't expect to "get much there." Her childhood friend Colleen didn't even talk to her anymore.

Even Aunt Ibby seemed dismissive of the woman. But maybe there was something more to Stasia than we were seeing behind the shapeless clothes, the dyed orange hair, the bubblegum. If there was, maybe I could find out what it was. Another thing Barbara's book advises is "listen for as long as you are interested." That's exactly what I intended to do.

By nine o'clock, showered, dressed and with notebook, pen and index cards in purse, I set out at a brisk walk for the Salem Common. I'd catch up with Aunt Ibby later to give her a full report on our late-night campfire adventure with the McKenna clan. I turned off my cell phone; I didn't want any interruptions if I could get the woman to open up to me.

I saw Stasia before I'd even crossed Washington Square. That orange hair was hard to miss. She sat on one of the benches at the perimeter of the Common, just inside the iron fence, the pink scooter parked beneath a nearby tree. She tossed bread crumbs from a brown paper bag to the congregation of cooing pigeons gathered around her feet and perched on the back of the bench. There was even one on her shoulder.

I hadn't considered that pigeon poop might be involved in this interviewing process, and wished I'd worn a hat. The woman looked up when I approached, her expression blank, inscrutable. It was hard to determine her age under that orange hair. *Older than me. Younger than Aunt Ibby,* I decided. *Fortyish?*

"Read your palm, ma'am? Tell your future?" She tossed what was left of the crumbs over her shoulder onto the ground behind the bench, thus dismissing the pigeons. She patted the bench beside her. "Grand

Duchess Stasia sees all." She smiled then, displaying small, even teeth, several of them capped in gold.

Trying not to look too closely at what I might be sitting in, I returned the smile and sat. "Thank you," I said. "I've never had my palm read before."

She gave me an up-and-down look, undoubtedly appraising how much I might be willing to pay to see into my future. I thought about that. The jeans and sweatshirt didn't hold much promise, but I was certain that she recognized the Frye boots and the Brahmin purse.

"Ten dollars okay?" Her voice was low, throaty. I'd expected some sort of an accent, but couldn't detect any.

"Okay," I said. "Which hand?"

"You right-handed?"

"Yes."

"Right hand to start." She took my hand in both of hers, turning mine over from back to front a couple of times, then smoothed my open palm with a gentle touch. She traced a line from just below my index finger toward my pinkie.

"You are content at the moment with your love life." It was a statement, not a question. I could only nod in agreement.

She touched a spot near the base of my ring finger. "Your heart was broken here. Sad. But it wasn't the man's fault. He died?"

Again I nodded.

"I'm sorry for that." She looked up from my palm, focusing brown eyes on mine. "I need to tell you that I know who you are. Your name is Lee Barrett. My reading of your hand is true and correct, but not because I already know some things about you."

I was surprised. Sure, I'd been trying to learn all I could about her, and even though I'd seen her a number of times lately, it hadn't occurred to me that she could be studying me at the same time. I quickly dismissed that thought. She'd probably recognized me from my short stint as a TV psychic.

"I know your name too," I admitted. "You're Stasia Novikova."

She leaned back against the bench, not letting go of my hand. "That's true. Everyone knows that."

"You told me just now that your name is Grand Duchess Stasia."

"True also."

"My grandfather Kowolski used to call me Princess Maralee." I smiled at the memory.

"Kozlovsky? Russian?" Her eyes widened.

"No. Kowolski. Polish."

"Polish. That's okay. My grandfather Novikova told me my true name was Grand Duchess Anastasia. I believed him. Everyone calls me Stasia, but my real name is Anastasia."

"Everyone calls me Lee," I told her.

Nodding, still smiling, she returned to the palm reading. "Your head line is long, deep." She tapped the line. "Your thinking is clear and focused. You must be a good teacher."

"I am a teacher. Did the palm tell you that or did you know?"

"Which do you think?"

Hey, wait a minute. Who's doing the interviewing here?

"I'd like to think you saw it in my palm."

"You'd be correct. It's there. And look here." She

tapped a curved semicircular line that started at the base of my thumb. "See how your fate line crosses your life line. Someone has given you great assistance in your life, from a very early age. Was it the grandfather?"

"No. My aunt." I wanted to get the conversation back to her. "I met an old friend of yours last night."

She frowned, not looking up from my hand. "Let me see the other hand now, Maralee. I don't have many friends. I don't need a lot of friends. My grandfather had the same five friends his whole life. But I'm curious. Who did you meet?"

I extended my left hand. "Colleen McKenna. I understand you were pen pals when you lived in . . . Where was it? Somewhere in Colorado?"

"Yes. Somewhere there. Look. This hand gives us a peek into your future. Your heart line says that you will become more free with expressing your emotions. You haven't yet been able to share your feelings completely. It will come, with time." She patted my hand. "Don't worry."

"You're a very interesting woman, Stasia," I said, testing my Barbara Walters philosophy. "I enjoyed the reading. Where did you learn to read palms?"

"Many Russian women can do it," she said. "It's not that difficult."

"I don't know much about Russian culture," I admitted. "I guess your grandfather was a strong influence in your life. Did he come here from Russia?"

She seemed to relax, letting go of my hand. "Yes. He arrived here in 1915. He was a carpenter in the court of the great Czar Nicholas II."

The Connecticut murdered man was a baker in the court of

Nicholas. "He must have been a very fine carpenter then, to have such an important position."

I saw the pride in her eyes. "He was wonderful. He could build anything. He was young, in his twenties, and already a master carver. Carved the royal crests on the czar's throne back in the old country."

"What an honor that must have been. Did he find similar work in America?"

"Nothing as grand as working in a palace, but he was happy here. He learned to carve likenesses of animals."

"Colleen and her brother remember your grand-father fondly. Your grandmother too."

"Grandmother Lydia. She was kind to me—before she grew old and sick and couldn't remember any-thing."

"Oh, that's so sad. I'm sorry."

She reached into a pocket and pulled out a pink square. She unwrapped it, popped the gum into her mouth, shrugged her shoulders and picked up my left hand again. "Yes. It was bad. She couldn't remember where she'd put anything. Even important things."

"She didn't remember you?"

"Nope. Didn't know anybody." She tapped my hand. "Listen. You be careful about relationships. You're too trusting." She shook her head. "Not like me. Not like me at all."

"I understand," I said. "I've heard that you're . . . well . . . a little bit reclusive."

She took a deep breath and blew an enormous bubble, then inhaled and made it disappear. I stared. If I'd done that, it would have popped and I'd have been picking gum out of my hair.

"You've probably heard that I'm a little bit crazy. Maybe I am." She held out her hand. "Ten dollars."

I reached for my purse, taking my time, searching for a way to keep the conversation going. But Grand Duchess Anastasia's face was once again expressionless. Without another word she tucked the ten-dollar bill I handed her into a pocket of the voluminous dress, and motioned to a woman passing by.

"Read your palm, ma'am? Tell your future?"

CHAPTER 16

I stood there for a moment, confused. Was I supposed to shake her hand, thank her for the reading, wish her a good day—what? The potential customer, with a negative shake of her head and a rather obvious side step to the outer edge of the path, hurried away. I figured I'd pretty much booted my first attempt at investigative-reporter interviewing. Too many questions still unanswered. I'd learned very little about Stasia, her grandparents or her interest in our storage locker acquisitions. Barbara had said to "Listen for as long as you are interested, and then a few minutes longer." Had I listened enough? Maybe I could give it one more shot.

I turned toward her and was met with a blank expression, a virtual thousand-yard stare. It was as though she hadn't the slightest idea who I was. Clearly, there'd be no more interviewing today. I decided I might as well fill out my index cards with what information I'd gathered and headed for the coffee shop on the corner of Essex Street.

I picked one of the smallest corner booths, bought a

small coffee, reluctantly passed on the cinnamon doughnut and pulled the notebook, pen and index cards from my purse. Notebook first. I'd scribble down everything I could remember, then sort it all out later and put it neatly onto the cards.

I began to write:

Stasia knew my name. I should have asked her how. It was probably because of the TV show. She knew I was a teacher too. Or did she? Maybe she really saw that in my palm. She's sticking to the Grand Duchess routine.

I paused, thinking about what I'd learned. *Her grandparents came here from Russia in 1915. Her grandfather had been a carpenter in the court of Czar Nicholas II. Her grandmother Lydia apparently suffered from dementia of some kind and didn't remember where she put things. She barely acknowledged that she knew Colleen. Admitted that she'd lived "somewhere in Colorado," but dodged the question of where. Says she's not a "trusting person."*

I chewed on the end of my pen for a moment, then wrote:

Is she the bubblegum-blowing crazy lady who reads palms on the Common, or is the whole thing a big act? Is Stasia an intelligent woman disguised as an eccentric Salem character? If so, why?

I wondered if Pete had found out anything about her that he could share. I reached for my phone and turned it back on. There was a voice mail from Pete.

"You busy? Call me when you get a chance. I've got

some artist's sketches of those two characters that grabbed your stuff from Goodwill."

That was something I was anxious to see. He answered on the first ring. "Hi, Lee. Where are you now? Home?"

"Nope. I'm in the coffee shop on the corner of Essex Street. You've got sketches, huh? Any ID?"

"Not yet. I'd like you to take a look though. Maybe you've seen them somewhere, or even if you haven't, I'll feel better if you know who we're dealing with. Will you be there for a few minutes? I can run over there with them."

"I'll be here. I was just getting my palm read, over on the Common."

"Stasia?"

"Uh-huh. I was practicing my interviewing skills while she told me my future."

"Learn anything interesting?"

"About me? Or Stasia?"

"Either one."

"I'll tell you when you get here. I'm making notes now."

For the next few minutes I read and re-read my notes, and at the same time looked back and forth, watching the door of the coffee shop, waiting for Pete to appear. It didn't take him long. He spotted me right away and slid into the narrow booth, putting a large manila envelope on the table.

"Here they are. I've already run it by the Goodwill people. They're all satisfied that these are good likenesses of the men they saw. Ready to take a look?"

"I'm ready."

Slowly he withdrew the first sketch from the envelope and laid it face up on the table. "How about this guy? Know him?"

I took my time. This was important, I knew. The man had a neatly trimmed beard. His hair was brown and so were his eyes. His complexion was what I'd call olive; his eyebrows were on the bushy side. He didn't look one bit familiar. "Sorry," I said. "Maybe if he didn't have the beard . . ."

"Never mind," Pete said, slipping the drawing back into the envelope and taking out the next sheet. "How about this one?"

I recognized the blond man right away. The artist had even drawn him wearing a black turtleneck, just like the one he'd worn when Aunt Ibby and I saw him at the storage locker auction.

I pointed. "This one. I recognize this one. He was at the storage locker auction."

"You sure?"

"I'm sure. He stood off to the side by himself. He didn't bid on anything while we were there. Lucky said he goes to all the auctions and never buys a thing."

"Lucky?"

"Just a man Aunt Ibby and I met at the auction. He goes to all of them and he said that one"—I tapped the picture—"is a regular at auctions, but never bids on anything. He said the same thing about Stasia, come to think of it. I'd better write that down." I reached for my notebook.

Pete put his hand over mine. "Write it down later. What else can you tell me about this guy? What was he wearing? Did you see him talking to anyone else? How can I get in touch with Lucky?"

I scribbled, *S. No bid,* so I wouldn't forget, and started to answer Pete's questions. I ticked them off on my fingers. "When I saw the blond man, he was all dressed in black. Black turtleneck, black jeans, black Nike sneakers. I didn't see him speak to anyone else. He stood by himself. Apart from the crowd."

"You sure he wasn't with Stasia?"

"He could have been with her, I suppose, but he wasn't standing near her, looking at her or speaking to her. Not that I saw."

"Okay. How about Lucky? Tell me about him."

"We call him Lucky because he was wearing a T-shirt with that word on it. But a woman there called him Lucky, so maybe that's really his nickname." I knew I wasn't being much help. "He told us a story about somebody who won a storage locker and found a corpse in a barrel inside it. Lucky said a man had murdered his wife and put her body in a barrel. It was discovered when the second wife didn't pay the locker rent."

"Probably true," Pete said. "I've heard of similar things happening more than once. Anything else?"

More than once? That's weird.

I thought about the auction, trying to remember our brief conversation with Lucky.

I snapped my fingers. "Hey. This might mean something. Lucky said that he hears about the locker auctions through ads and by e-mails from the auctioneer. Maybe the blond man is on the auctioneer's e-mail list too."

"Good one, Lee." He leaned over and kissed me on

the cheek. "Did I ever tell you you'd make a good cop? Thanks. Gotta go. Call you later."

Whoosh! He was gone. I grabbed a refill and got back to work on my notes:

> *Stasia didn't bid on anything. Was she in the habit of*
> *traveling around to storage locker auctions? Or just*
> *Salem auctions?*

I looked over my notes carefully. Had I missed something? I should have recorded it. I tried to play the conversation with Stasia back in my head, but nothing new emerged. With the notebook and pen back in my purse, the rubber band secured around the still-blank index cards, I started for home.

I walked down Oliver Street, which runs past our backyard, and pushed open the gate. I peeked in the garage window and noticed that the Buick was missing. Monthly library board meeting, no doubt. I hurried along the garden path to where O'Ryan waited for me on the back steps.

I unlocked the back door and together we hurried up the two flights. As soon as I'd entered the living room, I could tell that O'Ryan had been busy. Once again the Statue of Liberty pencil sharpener was on the floor—in the middle of the room this time, and beside it was the little bronzed skier. That one was a souvenir of a ski trip Johnny and I had taken to Vail. Vail, Colorado.

Stasia once lived somewhere in Colorado.

O'Ryan hopped up onto the zebra-striped chair and sat, watching me. I tossed my purse onto the couch and picked the pencil sharpeners up, holding one in each palm, balancing the two. "What do they mean, cat? What are you trying to tell me?"

He shook his big, fuzzy head from side to side, almost as though he couldn't believe anyone could be so obtuse, then jumped down from the chair and headed down the hall toward the kitchen. I put the pencil sharpeners back on top of the bookcase, then followed the cat. I wasn't too surprised when he walked right through the kitchen and trotted straight into the bedroom. No doubt I was in for another mirror-gazing session.

O'Ryan jumped onto the bed, turned around once, sat facing the mirror and looked at me. "Okay, cat. I get it." I gave him a gentle shove. "Move over." Together we faced the glass. The pinpoints of light, and then the swirling colors appeared. I wondered if he could see them too. I didn't feel the anxiety that usually accompanies the beginning of a vision. Maybe I was getting used to this strange "gift."

Once again, I was on the deck of a ship. Six men, with their backs to me, looked across the water to where, in the distance, Lady Liberty lifted her welcoming torch.

"Yes, I've seen this one before," I told the cat, much as though I was discussing the rerun of a TV show. "Aunt Ibby and I figured out that it's Nikita Novikova coming to America in 1915."

The man who'd smiled at me before turned and smiled again.

Hello, Nikita.

Then, turning slowly, one of the other men did the same.

The murdered baker from Connecticut came to America in 1915 too.

"Are you the baker?" I asked aloud.

The man tipped his hat, then faced the sea again.

The vision faded away. O'Ryan, circling behind me, jumped down from the bed and went back to the kitchen, leaving me wondering what I was supposed to learn from the rerun shipboard scene.

Not exactly a rerun.

So maybe Stasia's grandfather and the murdered baker had arrived in America on the same ship, on the same day. Who were the other four men? Were they people I needed to know about too?

At that moment I remembered something else Stasia had said. Something I hadn't written in the notebook.

"My grandfather had the same five friends his whole life."

CHAPTER 17

I knew then what we had to do and I could hardly wait for Aunt Ibby to get home from her library board meeting to help me get started. First we'd check vessels coming to Ellis Island from Russia during 1915. Next we'd check passenger lists. Find the Novikovas and the baker on the same ship. I had no idea how to go about doing that, but I was sure my tech-savvy aunt would have all the tools to get it done. According to my most recent vision, Grandpa Nick's five friends were important too. If they were all on board the same ship, and they'd been friends for his whole life, it's quite likely that they all came from the same place in Russia. Would my aunt be able to figure that out too? I had every confidence that she could.

The cuckoo announced eleven o'clock. If Aunt Ibby's meeting was of the usual duration, it would be over by now. Hoping she wouldn't elect to stay and help check out books, I hurried back to the living room, retrieved my purse and once again spread my growing collection of index cards on the kitchen counter. The cat resumed his draft-protecting role on the windowsill, eyes half closed.

Consulting my notebook, I began to fill in some fresh cards with the information I'd gleaned from my not-so-professional interview with Stasia, along with the conclusion I'd begun to draw from the morning's new mirror vision.

Abbreviating my notes, I filled out a few fresh cards. Maybe I'd learned more than I'd originally thought from Stasia. I added a question about Grandpa Nick and his five friends: *Did all six men work in the court of Czar Nicholas II?*

I thought about the pencil sharpeners and added another card: *Colorado is connected to the people arriving in New York. (O'Ryan thinks so.)*

I replaced the rubber band and looked with some satisfaction at the growing stack. I smiled at the cat. It was all beginning to make some sense. Not a great deal of sense to be sure, but some.

Now, if my aunt will just hurry up and get home, we can start connecting the dots.

Cuckoo announced eleven-thirty. As though on cue, O'Ryan jumped from his perch and raced down the hall toward the living room. I heard the small clicking noise the cat door makes when he's in a hurry. Good. That meant she must be home.

I followed the cat and by the time I'd reached the first-floor back hall, I heard the garage door closing. O'Ryan was already outside. I unlocked the door and joined him on the brick steps. Aunt Ibby pushed open the garden gate and waved to us. "What's this? A reception committee?"

"It is," I said. "We could hardly wait for you to get here. I have so much to tell you."

"I have exciting news too," she said, joining us on the back steps. "Let's get inside and compare notes."

"Perfect. I have real notes to compare. You'll be proud of me. They're all neatly written on index cards." I followed her into the hall and stood aside, waiting for her to fish the keys out of her purse and to unlock the kitchen door.

"Such efficiency," she said, "and I'm always proud of you." She tapped her forehead. "My notes are still up here." O'Ryan, my aunt and I stepped into the warm, cozy room. It smelled of gingerbread.

"My cards are upstairs," I said. "I'll run up and get them."

"Good. I'll change out of my librarian clothes and meet you back here in a jiffy."

I guess a "jiffy" in our house is something like Tabitha Trumbull's a "pinch" or a "dab." In this case it was time enough for me to swap the too-warm sweatshirt and the too-fancy boots for a Bruins T-shirt and sneakers, to grab the index cards and hurry back downstairs. Aunt Ibby, in flowered cotton, waited at the round oak table. I'm used to seeing surprises on that table—usually of the edible variety, but this time the surprise was unexpected. In the center of the table was the samovar, in all its gleaming glory. It was displayed on my great-grandmother Forbes's huge sterling-silver serving tray and flanked by Grandmother Russell's best antique Gorham coin silver sugar bowl and creamer.

"Wow!" I said. "Are we expecting the royal family for

tea?" I sat opposite her, trying to peek over and around the glitzy display.

"Not exactly," she said, beaming. "But doesn't it look impressive?"

"Sure does. I guess this has something to do with your exciting news?"

"I could hardly wait to get home to tell you about it. I've come up with a grand idea for funding the book-mobile, and this morning the board approved it!"

For years Aunt Ibby's been part of every fund-raising effort for a special bookmobile to serve the children of Salem's low-income neighborhoods. Apparently, her new big idea involved our family-heirloom silver—and included the samovar. "Tell me about it," I said.

"High tea," she said, "at the library. It's going to be the social event of the fall season. Everybody who is any-body is going to be there. Think of it, Maralee! Cream scones and tiny fairy cakes and madeleines! Dainty, little sandwiches! Truffled egg salad with cress! Oh, my dear, can't you just picture it?"

Her enthusiasm was contagious. "It sounds amazing," I agreed. "But you're not Superwoman. You're not actu-ally planning to prepare the food, as well as chair the event, I hope."

"Good heavens, no." Her smile grew even broader. "It'll be a real English high tea. I'm planning to have Harrods cater."

"Harrods? The London Harrods?"

"The one and only. You remember my friend Nigel St. John?"

"Of course. Nigel of New Scotland Yard." She pro-nounced his last name as "Sin Jin." Though I'd never met Nigel, I knew he was a "gentleman friend" of my aunt's. Exactly what their history was, I didn't know—didn't want to know—but Nigel had been extremely helpful to us a year or so earlier when we'd needed some accurate overseas information. "What about him?"

"You know that Nigel and I chat online occasionally, even on the telephone every so often." I hadn't known that, but nodded agreement. "Well, I told him about the tea and he suggested that we order everything from Harrods. He's volunteered to pick it up and get an early flight to Boston on the day of the event!"

"Nigel is going to carry by hand your truffles and fairy cakes and scones, all the way from England?"

An unruffled, ladylike shrug of one shoulder. "Of course he is. What are friends for?"

"You're a wonder," I said. "When will this event take place?"

"Next month. We've ordered the engraved invitations and Mrs. Abney-Babcock—you remember her? Louisa Abney-Babcock, the president of the library board? She's graciously offered to lend us her great-grandmother's double set of Canton china for the occasion."

"More than gracious, I'd say. That set must be worth a fortune."

"Priceless, I agree. But you have news too. Tell me everything."

"This may take a while. I've had a busy day." I gave a little pinkie wave over the assembled silver. "Could we sit somewhere else? All this reflective stuff is kind of distracting."

"Oh, dear. I didn't even think of that. Come on." She stood. "Let's sit in the dining room." She led the way, with the cat and me following. I was happy to get away from the mirrorlike silver surfaces, even though there'd been no prevision swirls or sparkles in evidence at all. I placed my stack of cards on the long dining-room table and sat opposite my aunt. O'Ryan made himself comfortable on the needlepoint cushion on the chair next to me.

"I'll start with last night," I said. "When Pete and I left for the movies, it was so pleasant outside that we decided to walk." I traced our steps for her, told her about seeing the McKenna family in their yard and about how we'd joined them for s'mores. Taking the rubber band from my cards, I read aloud from the ones that referred to information the McKennas had given us.

"Colleen McKenna and Stasia were pals when they were kids," I read. My aunt was clearly surprised.

"Now, that's interesting," she said. "Are they still friends? Now that Stasia lives here?"

"No, they're not," I told her, "and maybe that's even more interesting. But I'm getting ahead of my story. I talked to Stasia today."

"But . . . how . . . ?" I could almost see the questions forming in her mind.

"I'll get to it. Don't worry. I found out that Stasia lived 'somewhere in Colorado.' I thought maybe we could check the census reports and maybe learn something about what was going on with the Novikovas back then."

She nodded, smiling. "We can do that. Can hardly wait to get going on this. What fun!"

"Okay. That's about all I learned from the McKennas. Except that they all seem to have saved some gifts Nikita and Lydia gave to them. Colleen has an embroidered tablecloth and a matryoshka, and her mother has the most amazing nested Easter eggs. I grabbed a cell phone picture of it for you."

"You say you've actually talked to Stasia?"

"I did. This morning. Walked over to the Common, had my palm read and practiced my amateur interviewing skills."

"And . . . ?"

I fanned out the cards. "Stasia says her grandparents came to America from Russia in 1915. Grandfather was a carpenter, a wood-carver, important in the court of Czar Nicholas II. Lydia was kind to her, but apparently suffered from some sort of dementia in later years. Stasia seemed quite agitated about that."

I found myself talking faster and faster, anxious to get everything in. I told her about Chief Whaley's newspaper clippings and the murdered baker in Connecticut. I described the artist's drawings of the trash stealers too, and how I'd recognized the blond man. Finally, out of breath, I leaned back in my chair. "I'm sure I've left some things out, but, anyway, this pretty much catches you up on where I am on all of this."

"On this 'caper'?" Her grin was wide and contagious. She clasped her hands together. "This is so exciting. An excellent adventure." Her expression grew serious. "I mean, except for poor Eric Dillon dying like that. How's Pete doing with the investigation? Any progress there?"

"I don't know for sure, but Scott Palmer said this morning that they'd be holding a presser at noon today." I checked my watch. "It's time. Want to go into the den and see what's going on?"

"Let's go." She beat me to the den and already had

the remote in her hand when I got there. *Click*. There was Scott with the police station in the background. He'd managed to position himself right in front of the lectern they'd set up for the chief. I had to admit he was getting pretty good at his job.

Scott spoke in the hushed tones the announcers at golf tournaments use. "We're expecting Chief Whaley within a few minutes. He'll be updating us on any progress that's been made on the Eric Dillon murder. As you know, Dillon was an investigative reporter and the writer of a series of popular books on the subject of treasure hunting. He was working on a new book before his untimely death. Oh, here comes Chief Whaley now. Stay tuned to WICH-TV, folks, always first with the news on Boston's North Shore."

The chief, in dress uniform complete with star and medals, approached the lectern. Looking uncomfortable, he adjusted the microphone and put a couple of sheets of paper on the lectern.

"He doesn't look happy," Aunt Ibby said.

"Pete says the chief hates these public-speaking things," I told her. "He gets through them as fast as he can, and answers as few questions as he can get away with."

Chief Whaley cleared his throat. "Ladies and gentlemen, it's been brought to my attention that some people in Salem, especially those in the neighborhood where Mr. Dillon's death took place, are afraid that this was a random killing, and that they may be in danger too. We have reason to believe that Mr. Dillon personally was targeted and that the public at large is not in any danger. This is not to say that you should be careless.

Lock the doors in your homes and your vehicles. Our department is working aggressively to bring this case to a close. If you have information about Mr. Dillon, his whereabouts on the night of his death, or any companions you may have seen him with, call the number at the bottom of your screen." He lifted the piece of paper from the lectern. "I have here two artist's sketches to show you. Please bear in mind that these men are not suspected of any wrongdoing whatsoever. We think that one or both of them may have some information that may be important to this case."

He held the papers up, one in each hand, displaying the artist's sketches Pete had shown to me. "If you see either of these men, please don't approach them. Just call the number at the bottom of your screen. That's all for now. Thank you." He took one hesitant step away from the microphone before the questions began.

A reporter shouted, "Let's get a better look at those pictures, Chief!"

"Okay. There are printed copies available to all of you inside the station." He held the pictures up again and the camera moved in.

"Those are the pictures Pete showed you, aren't they?" my aunt asked, leaning closer to the screen. "I remember that blond man. He was at the sale. And the bearded man. I've seen him before too."

"Really? He doesn't look familiar to me at all. Where did you see him?"

"It was quite a while ago. Over a year. Maybe even two. Let me think."

I watched the hand-waving reporters, listened to a few more shouted questions.

"What about the murder weapon? Have you found it?"

"Was anything stolen from the furniture shop?"

"Fingerprints?"

The chief walked toward the relative safety of the police station, his answers terse. "No prints. Carbone says nothing's gone. Weapon's still missing."

The camera once again focused on Scott, who briefly recapped what the chief had said, then turned the program back to Phil Archer in the studio. Aunt Ibby hit the MUTE button. "Didn't learn anything new, did we? Except that they don't think it was a random killing."

"You know, it looked like one," I said. "Robbers being interrupted by somebody peeking in the window. Killing him so he wouldn't identify them."

"You're right. How do they know it wasn't exactly that?"

"I don't know," I admitted. "There's a lot Pete doesn't tell me."

CHAPTER 18

Aunt Ibby and I were at Shaw's Market in the pet food aisle when she suddenly stopped the cart and snapped her fingers. "I've got it," she said. "I remember."

I looked down at the shopping list in my hand, pretty sure we hadn't forgotten anything. "Remember what?"

"His beard was much longer then, bushier too, but I'm pretty sure it was the same man."

"The artist's sketches?"

"Yes."

"Who is he?" I reached for my phone. "Should I call Pete?"

"I don't know *who* he is. I just remember where I saw him. He was at the library and he asked me for help. He was researching . . . something."

"Can you remember what it was? Might be important."

"I'm trying." I recognized the look she gets when she's concentrating, so I studied the shopping list silently and tossed things into the cart as we moved up and down the aisles. She didn't speak again until we reached the toy aisle. "Got it," she said. "He wanted information on amusement parks. Yes, That was it. Amusement parks."

"Local amusement parks? Or amusement parks in general?"

"Historic parks. He was interested in the old ones. Especially the one at the Salem Willows. He was a little difficult to understand. Strong foreign accent."

"The Willows? Where the carousel is?"

"Right. We didn't have a lot on it. He was mostly interested in old photos of the place, as I recall. I suggested that he go down to the Essex Institute to see what they might have."

"Did you ever see him again? Did he come back?"

She shook her head. "He was from out of town. I remember that because he didn't have a library card. Never saw him again."

"Ms. Foster at the Goodwill store said that one of those trash stealers had an accent. Anyway, if you saw him, so did other people. Someone must know who he is."

We moved through the checkout line, where I added a copy of *Car and Driver* and a Mounds bar to the groceries on the moving belt. Aunt Ibby handed the woman behind the cash register several canvas bags, and with bags full we headed for the car. "You know, Maralee," she said, "things just keep getting more and more complicated ever since we bought that locker—and the more we learn, the more complicated everything seems to get."

"You've got that right," I agreed. "Let's do something

uncomplicated this afternoon, something that can't possibly get us into any trouble."

"Good one. Let's hurry home, put this stuff away and plan the rest of our day. I have a good idea brewing too."

With the groceries safely stashed in our respective kitchens, Aunt Ibby and I repaired once again to her living room. I hadn't come up with any particularly original thoughts, and since she'd already said that she had an idea, I waited for her to tell me about it.

"Here's my thought," she said. "Since we seem to be involved with things Russian, and since I'm in the throes of planning a high tea, what do you say we combine the two?"

"Fine. How do we do that?"

"We take afternoon tea at that new place, the Russian Tea Experience, around the corner from St. Vladimir's."

"Perfect," I said. "I've never been there. Have you?"

"No, although I've been meaning to. I thought maybe I could add some Russian goodies to the menu to complement the samovar. Maybe even add some Russian touches to the table decorations."

"Good idea. Maybe you could use some of Grandpa Nick's carved toys."

"We're thinking along the same lines," she said. "Let's put on some going-to-tea clothes and do this."

So that's what we did—me in crinkle skirt and white blouse, and Aunt Ibby in hunter-green pantsuit. We set out in my car for an uncomplicated afternoon pastime that couldn't possibly get us into any trouble.

for my show. Rhonda's still the receptionist, and Wanda still does the weather. Nothing changes much around there." She lowered her voice and glanced around the room. "Marty says something's going on with Scott and Pete. She saw Scott getting into Pete's car one afternoon. You know anything about it?"

"I do, but I don't think I should say anything right now. Don't worry though. I'm sure it's nothing to worry about."

"It's okay. I understand. Dating a cop means you have to keep quiet about some things. Same as reading cards or tea leaves. I don't tell everything I see."

"Speaking of things occult, I had my palm read yesterday."

"No kidding? Don't tell me you had Stasia read you."

"I did. And she may not be as—um—strange as she looks."

"How was the reading? As good as mine?" She pouted prettily, and put down her fork.

"Of course not, silly. Very basic. She admitted she knew who I was and already had some information about me anyway. I guess it was from watching *Nightshades*. I think I learned more about her than she did about me." I told River about Grandpa Nick and naturally that led to the story about Pete and me crashing the McKennas' backyard party.

"You *have* been busy, haven't you?"

"That's nothing. I haven't even got to the part about the Russian Tea Experience and my aunt dating a 'person of interest.'" I looked at my watch. "But it's getting late. I'll save that story for next time. You have to get to work."

We both passed on having dessert. River got a coffee to go. "I need something to keep me awake through the movie," she said, picking up the red velvet cape she'd tossed over the back of her chair.

"I see Ariel's collection of velvet capes is still useful."

She settled the soft fabric around her bare shoulders. "Yes. I like wearing them. Warm and comfy, and I like that they were Ariel's, you know? Her being a fellow witch and all."

Enough talk about witches!

"I'll walk back to the station with you," I said. "I parked in the employee lot. Hope nobody minds." We split the check and the tip and began the short walk along Derby Street to WICH-TV's waterfront office block. River hurried up the steps, tapped a code into the security panel and pushed the heavy front door open.

"Good night, Lee. If you want to watch the show, the movie is *The Ship of Monsters*. A real classic!"

I laughed and headed around the corner of the old brick building. "Thanks anyway. I'll watch your intro, but I'll probably pass on the scary, old movie." The lot was nearly empty at that time of night. I could see my 'Vette, silhouetted against moonlit Salem Harbor at the rear of the station property. I hastened my steps, regretting my decision to park in my onetime assigned space close to the back door of the TV studio, adjacent to the granite seawall that held some bad memories for me.

Lighting was dim. No surprise there. Bruce Doan, the station manager, was notoriously thrifty, and adequate outside lighting had never been one of his priorities. I squinted into the darkness, sensing a slight motion beside the automobile. I stopped walking and stood still,